ANNIE'S CASTLE BY THE SEA

After a lifetime of putting her daughter first, widowed Annie travels to the beautiful Italian island of Vescovina for a summer. Annie's soon swept up in the magic of the place, but when the town is under threat by developers it's up to Annie and her gorgeous new friend, Giovanni, to save it. But as pressure begins to mount, is it really the town that needs saving — or Annie's heart?

CHRISTINA GARBUTT

$\blacklozenge$

ANNIE'S CASTLE BY THE SEA

Complete and Unabridged

LINFORD
Leicester

First published in Great Britain in 2019

First Linford Edition
published 2021

A catalogue record for this book is available
from the British Library.

ISBN 978–1–4448–4736–9

Published by
Ulverscroft Limited
Anstey, Leicestershire

Printed and bound in Great Britain by
TJ Books Ltd., Padstow, Cornwall

This book is printed on acid-free paper

1

'I'm so glad you're finally here,' said Tilly, throwing her arms around Annie and squeezing her tightly. For a small woman she had amazing strength and Annie struggled to breathe as she hugged her aunt back. 'It's taken you an absolute age to arrive.'

Annie smiled at her aunt's dramatic welcome. It had only been two weeks since she'd received her aunt's letter inviting her to come to Italy to help her with her latest project.

Tilly pushed Annie away, her colourful bracelets jangling, and held her at arm's length.

'You're looking well,' she observed. 'A bit on the skinny side and definitely too pale, but we can sort that out.'

'Tilly, I've only just stepped off the plane and you're already nagging me!' Annie laughed.

'I'm merely telling you how it is. Now

let's find ourselves a taxi and you can tell me all your news. How is Molly settling in at university?'

Tilly tucked her arm companionably through Annie's and steered her out of the tiny airport. Annie was content to follow her lead. It was a long time since someone had mothered her, and she enjoyed the sensation of being taken care of. She and Tilly hadn't been alone together for any considerable time for ages. Not since Annie's beloved childhood sweetheart had died, leaving Annie a widow at twenty-five and a single mother of an adorable but heartbroken four-year-old.

Tilly had stepped in and taken care of Annie until she was able to stand on her own two feet again, and Annie loved her for it.

Glancing at them, no one would immediately think they were related. Where Annie was tall and fair, Tilly was short with a dark complexion. Only their thick blonde hair was the same — but whereas Tilly grew hers long and wove it with ribbons and beads, Annie's was

2

shoulder length and often pulled back in a stubby ponytail.

Outside the sun was still warm and Annie breathed in the unfamiliar scents. She hadn't been abroad in six years, and this was only her third time out of the UK in her life. The air felt different from home — heavier and more pungent.

A handful of taxis were lined up in a designated bay but the drivers were all out chatting to one another and no one seemed in a hurry to come and take Annie and Tilly where they wanted to go.

'Yoo—hoo,' called Tilly, enthusiastically waving to the assembled drivers. 'We'd like a lift to Castello di Giacobbella per favore.'

The tallest driver unpeeled himself from the group and smilingly took Annie's suitcase. He dumped it into the boot of the nearest taxi and the women clambered in.

The warm leather seat was sticky under Annie's short skirt. She wound down the window, keen to get some air moving through the stuffy car.

'You're going to love it here,' declared Tilly as they left the confines of the airport and pulled onto a dual carriageway. 'The air is so fresh and the scenery is breathtaking. And the locals — they are so friendly. I honestly think that this time I've found my forever home.'

Annie grinned as she turned to look out of the window. Tilly was always finding her 'forever home'. Annie wasn't convinced Tilly would stay here any longer than she had at the cactus farm or living in a yurt in rural France. But for once, she could see what appealed to Tilly so much. The flat landscape around the airport quickly gave way to rolling hills dotted with squat olive trees. In the distance she could just make out the shimmering opal-blue sea. It was paradise.

'Tell me about your hotel,' said Annie as she gazed at the changing scenery.

'Best you see it for yourself, darling. I don't want to spoil it with an inadequate description. But I will tell you that it's set

4

just above a little town called Vescovina, which is a dear place full of character. It's not a touristy part of the island and the main income is the fantastic olive trees you see everywhere. Olive-picking season has just finished, which was a remarkable experience.'

'If the area is not touristy, how will you attract guests?' asked Annie, not worrying too much. Tilly had asked Annie, with her eye for artistic detail, for some help. Annie was guessing she'd be in Italy for a couple of weeks helping Tilly with the finishing touches to her hotel before returning home. What she was going to do then was another matter; Annie brushed that thought aside. She would worry about it when it happened.

'My hotel will be boutique. I might offer special weeks like a yoga or writing retreat, which will attract people who enjoy the quiet life. I haven't finalised the details yet, darling, but trust me when I say it is going to be fabulous.'

'How could anything out here not be wonderful?' said Annie, uncharacteristically emotional.

Tilly grinned and patted Annie's knee. 'I think this is going to be the making of you,' she said, much to Annie's surprise. She considered herself to be 'made' already.

The taxi thundered past a signpost to Vescovina and began a tortuous ascent up a steep, narrow road. Over the worryingly loud grinding of gears Tilly shouted, 'We're nearly there.'

After five very long minutes the taxi juddered to a halt and, open-mouthed, Annie stepped out.

'It's a castle,' she said. 'A real-life castle.' 'Welcome to Castello di Giocobbella,' said Tilly, her voice full of pride.

'It's so beautiful,' Annie breathed. 'It's just so ...' She flapped her hands, lost for words.

When Tilly had given the taxi driver their address it hadn't occurred to her that the castello was an actual castle. She'd imagined an old, traditional hotel given the name *castello* to make it seem grander than it actually was.

But she was wrong.

The driver had deposited them at the corner of the building. It wasn't particularly big, maybe the width of three detached houses. Annie wasn't sure if it properly counted as a castle because of its diminutive size but there was a round tower, and battlements ran along the top.

Annie took a few steps and touched the bleached stones of the castle wall. Thick leaves covered the base of the building and a rough mud path ran alongside. It was beautiful.

'Look at those arched windows,' she said breathlessly. 'I bet the view from them is stunning.'

'You'll get a better view of the surrounding area from the front. We're so high up, you can see for miles,' said Tilly, picking up Annie's suitcase and wheeling it towards the path. 'Come on.'

'Wow — this is amazing, Tilly,' said Annie as the view opened up in front of them. Her senses were overwhelmed by all the beauty around her. To their right, hills covered with green vegetation spread as far as she could see. To the left, a steep path led down towards the sea.

'Are those Roman ruins?' she asked, pointing in the direction of the sea where she could just make out what looked like a series of stone walls emerging from a small area of pine woodland.

'They could be. I haven't had time to venture down there yet,' admitted Tilly.

Annie stood for a few more minutes breathing deeply and taking in the view. Then she turned slowly back to the castle.

'What's the tent for?' she asked as she spotted the brightly coloured fabric a few metres away from the castle entrance.

'All will be revealed,' said Tilly cryptically.

'I can't wait to see inside. Shall we go in?' asked Annie enthusiastically.

Tilly tilted her head to one side. 'Um, yes, let's do that in a minute. Is there anything else you want to look at outside first?'

'I don't think so,' said Annie, turning

back to the view. 'Unless there's something you think I would particularly like to see.'

'Er, well there's quite a bit of land attached to the castle. That's pretty lovely. We could go and take a look at that.'

'Maybe later. I'd like to see inside now,' Annie insisted. Why was Tilly being so strange?

Tilly took a deep breath and nodded. 'OK, yes, let's do that then. Come on.'

Tilly headed through an archway. Annie followed. As a child she'd always dreamed of living in a castle and a tingle of excitement shot down her spine as she stepped into the stone building.

It took a moment for her eyes to adjust to the darkness. She stood, staring at everything before her. And just like that, the fairytale was over.

'It's a ruin,' she stated, taking in the exposed walls and piles of rubble.

'Not exactly,' said Tilly, a little sheepishly. 'There is a roof, and I'm pretty sure it's stable.'

'Pretty sure it's... I hope it's definitely stable! We don't want to get crushed to death in our sleep.'

'Ah, well.' Tilly paused. 'That's what the tent is for.'

'Pardon?' demanded Annie.

'The tent. We'll have to sleep in that for a while but you like camping, don't you?'

'Only for the odd weekend now and again,' said Annie, fighting a strange urge to giggle.

Tilly stopped to take that in.

'Oh. I see. Well, it won't be for that long. I've employed a foreman and he tells me that as soon as they've sorted out the walls they'll be able to run the wires for the electricity.'

'There's no electricity? At least tell me there's running water.'

'Not in the hotel, but there is a very lovely stream nearby and it's private so we can wash in there.' Tilly's voice was high with false jolliness.

That was too much. Annie burst out laughing. 'When you said you needed help with refurbishing the place I thought you meant choosing colour schemes and deciding on fabrics for cushions. I didn't imagine I'd be living rough miles away from anywhere,' she managed to get out between gusts of laughter.

Tilly grinned sheepishly.

'I didn't want to put you off coming.'

Annie reached over and pulled her aunt into a hug, 'I'll always come when you ask. Don't worry about me; it'll be a fabulous adventure but we do need to talk about what my role is going to be, because it's totally different to how I imagined.'

Tilly hugged her back.

'I do have a proposition for you — but shall we talk business tomorrow? Tonight I'd like to catch up with my favourite niece.'

'If there's your company, some good food and wine, then I'm happy.'

'Excellent.' Tilly's shoulders sagged in relief.

Annie chuckled and looked around at the piles of rubble and dust. She needn't have hauled her heavy suitcase through customs after all. Her wash bag full of luxury shampoo and conditioner was mostly redundant — but what an adventure lay ahead of her!

2

Annie followed the stream as it raced over rocks and twisted round corners, trying to find a spot deep and private enough to bathe in.

The water meandered along for about a mile until it widened into a natural pool. The water seemed to rest there for a while before continuing its journey downstream.

Annie's skin felt slick with clamminess and she didn't want anyone to stand near her until she'd been able to wash, in case she smelled as bad as she felt. The silvery water twinkled invitingly in the early morning sun — but how cold would it be?

Annie dipped her toes in and whipped them back out quickly. The water was freezing.

'Pull yourself together, Annie,' she muttered.

She stripped off her dress and adjusted

the straps on her bikini. Her stomach was smooth with only faint, silvery stretch marks over her hips to suggest she'd ever been pregnant.

'Right — I'm going to do this.'

She stood on the bank of the river, flexing her fingers and puffing out her cheeks. Before she could think about it too much, she stepped in and knelt down until her shoulders were covered.

'Aaah!' she called out. 'It's so cold.'

She grabbed the bar of soap she'd left on the bank and quickly rubbed it over herself. Within seconds she was done and climbing gratefully out of the water.

Her skin dried quickly under the warm sun. She hadn't been able to face dipping her head under the water, and so she pulled her hair back into a short ponytail. She tied a sarong around her and began to make her way back to the castle.

She wasn't sure what she was supposed to do. She'd been at a bit of a loose end after Molly had left for university and she'd so welcomed Tilly's invitation to

Italy to take her mind off the emptiness of their little house.

Was being at a loose end in Italy any better than feeling that way at home?

The dip in the stream had certainly woken her up. She'd needed it; she and Tilly had sat up until the early hours of the morning discussing everything and nothing.

Annie had realised how much she'd missed her beloved aunt over the last few years. They'd been so close when Annie was younger with Annie living with her for long periods of time while her own parents had travelled for work. Then Tilly had moved in with her after the death of Hugo, and stayed until she was able to cope on her own.

Not only was Tilly family, she was one of Annie's best friends.

As they'd sat chatting, Annie had gazed at the castle bathed in silvery moonlight which softly lit up its craggy walls, and she'd fallen in love with the enchanting ruin. She'd been surprised that the feeling had stayed with her, even in the bright light of the morning, with the castle revealed as not much more than a shell rather than something magical out of a fairytale.

The reassuring sound of power tools filled the air as Annie neared the tent. She turned a corner and saw several vans parked haphazardly at the entrance to the castle.

Deciding to leave well alone for the moment Annie set about finding what, if anything, there was for breakfast. Opening a wicker basket, she discovered a hunk of bread and some fruit. She tore off a chunk from the loaf and chose a couple of ripe-looking pears.

Leaning against the wall of the castle, she looked down towards the ruins in the distance. Whatever the day held, she was going to make exploring them a priority.

'There you are,' said Tilly, emerging from a nearby archway. 'I was about to send out a search party in case you'd lost your way. You've missed the most thrilling morning. The building inspector's been and has signed off the integrity of the building as safe. Not long after he left, the foreman and some of his workers arrived.'

Tilly was vibrating with contagious excitement. 'That's great news. How long will it take before we have electricity and water?'

'Oh, not long,' said Tilly breezily.

'How long is 'not long'?' Annie pushed.

'Well, it's difficult to say because we have to have some of the walls taken down and others channelled and plastered and everything — but it will be soon.'

Annie nodded. She still wasn't sure what her role was. It wasn't as if she could wield power tools. She was handier than most with a drill but there was probably more to renovation than putting up curtain poles, which was her main drilling experience.

'How many people are here?' she asked.

'Four. Six if you include us.'

'Have we any food to give them?' asked Annie, her maternal instincts kicking in.

'Not really. Would you mind popping

to the town and getting some?' asked Tilly apologetically.

Annie smiled. 'You mustn't feel you can't ask me to do things. You are paying me to work and I'd rather be busy than wondering what to do.'

Tilly frowned. 'I don't want you to feel I'm being bossy.'

'You're always bossy.' Annie grinned.

Tilly laughed her big, boisterous laugh and Annie smiled at her aunt as she tucked into her second pear. The juice ran down her chin and she wiped it away with the back of her hand.

'There's money for food in the bag under my camping bed,' said Tilly. 'To get to the town, you need to head down the path that's round the back of the castle. It's quite steep to begin with but it levels out fairly quickly. It's a bit punishing on the way back up, but the walk will keep us fit.'

Annie finished her pear and pushed herself away from the wall.

'When you get back we'll have a serious chat about your role here and what I need you to do,' Tilly continued.

'OK,' said Annie, glad that Tilly had given some thought to what help she needed. She didn't want to feel like a spare wheel.

'And you don't have to worry about one thing,' said Tilly as she began to head back through the archway from which she'd come.

'What's that?'

'You're definitely going to be kept busy.' Annie laughed as she disappeared from sight.

★ ★ ★

Grabbing a backpack and a handful of the euros she found under Tilly's bed, as well as some of her own in case anything in the town took her fancy, Annie dug her phone out from where she'd ditched it after frustrated attempts to find a signal.

Heading towards Vescovina, she held her phone in her hand and checked for a signal every few metres. The thought of not being able to contact Molly for the weeks she was here terrified her.

But it was even worse thinking that her daughter may not be able to contact her. Anything could happen to her while Annie was away...

The steep path that led down to the town had just started to level out when her phone finally pinged to life. Molly's message was brief.

I'm having a great time. You must stop worrying about me. Have you managed to get any tan on your pasty white legs yet? xxx

She smiled as she replied.

No tan yet but I'm working on it. Miss you already. Speak to you soon, love, Mum xxx

Message done, she slipped her phone into the front of her backpack and carried on walking.

She passed fields packed tightly with

neat rows of vines. She peered closer and saw that the branches were heavy with grapes. A wave of longing for a long, cold glass of wine swept over her. She mentally added a bottle to her shopping list, along with a bag of ice to keep the wine cool long enough for her to enjoy it. She turned a corner and could at last see Vescovina emerging from the hilly countryside. She sped up, keen to explore the interesting-looking town.

Eventually the path she was following came out into a narrow alleyway between two tall buildings. She ran her fingers over the light-red brick of the building nearest her. Tilly had told her the town was medieval, but she hadn't realised how beautiful the stone would be.

At the end of the alleyway she emerged onto a wide cobblestone avenue, flanked with shops tightly packed together. Most of the buildings were the same almost-pink colour as the first building she'd seen, although here they were interspersed with whitewashed stone. Rickety balconies poked out across the street and archways led off in different directions. Old men sat in groups, some playing cards, others talking and gesticulating. The effect was picture-book perfect.

Annie was looking for Carlotta's, a store Tilly raved about, which should be on this main street. She set off in the direction Tilly had told her to go. She meandered down the road spending time nosing in all the shops and studying the menus of the cafés which spilled out onto the pavement. She bought a wide, floppy straw hat to protect herself from the sun.

Eventually she came across a green awning displaying the name *Carlotta's* in bold letters. The store was one of the pale cream buildings and looked as if it had recently been given a lick of paint, unlike those on either side of it which were beautiful but shabby.

She pushed her way in and let the door close softly behind her. Inside was a quiet, cool haven. Behind the counter a woman stood, flicking through a magazine, her dark hair escaping from a messy bun. She glanced up at Annie standing just inside the doorway and smiled warmly.

Annie was struck by the woman's unusual, light blue eyes against her dark skin. She smiled back and picked up a metal basket.

She moved towards an area where fresh fruit was stacked high in square containers. Large, oddly shaped peppers were stacked next to plump aubergines and she began to fill the basket with whatever took her fancy.

She vaguely heard the shop door open and heavy boots moving across the shop floor. She rounded the end of another aisle and found the meats and cheeses. A quick-flowing conversation was going on near the counter. She could just make out the light voice of the shopkeeper and the deeper rumble of her visitor. Nothing they said was comprehensible to Annie.

Annie had never learned Italian — an oversight she was now regretting.

She added packets of sliced ham to her basket and some thin slices of pale, creamy cheese. How was she going to communicate with anyone when she didn't understand the language? Why hadn't she bought even something simple like a guidebook with common phrases? She'd decided to leave Britain so quickly that she hadn't given enough thought to the practicalities.

She threw a few more things into her basket. Hopefully she could get away with nodding and smiling. Paying shouldn't be a problem, because she could look at the numbers on the till. If the shopkeeper tried to talk to her, she could apologise in English and look as contrite as possible. She couldn't believe she hadn't thought about the language barrier until this moment.

She was so lost in her panic that she didn't notice she wasn't alone in her aisle any more.

She took a step back and collided with something solid. She spun round and ended up hitting Carlotta's only other customer with her basket, which flew out of her hands on impact and her shopping scattered over the floor.

'Aaah!' yelled the man. 'Mi hai fatto proprio male.'

Annie watched in dismay as several oranges bounced away and rolled under the display cabinets. The eggs she'd carefully chosen cracked and oozed over the shop floor. The urge to flee was almost overwhelming.

The man was still muttering darkly as she scrabbled around trying to gather up the contents of her basket.

'I'm so sorry,' she stuttered.

As she moved across the shop floor she inadvertently stepped on the man's foot. She gasped in surprise and immediately straightened, knocking the top of her head into his chin.

She staggered and the man grabbed the tops of her arms holding her steady.

'Stai cercando di uccidermi?' he growled. She gazed up at him uncomprehendingly.

He glared down at her, his eyebrows a thick, dark slash above fierce blue eyes.

'Umm,' she murmured. 'I'm désolée.

I'm very, very désolée.'

He held her arms for a moment longer and then slowly released her.

'Désolée,' she said again, unable to think under his intense scrutiny.

His lips twitched even as his scowl remained. 'The words you're looking for,' he said in perfect English but with a thick Italian accent, 'are 'mi dispiace.' 'Désolée' is French.'

Before she could say anything else he swept past her and out of the shop, the door slamming shut after him.

Tears of humiliation threatened as she bent down and continued to gather up her goods. She was aware of footsteps but dared not look up.

'That,' said a woman's voice, which was also heavily accented, 'was very funny.'

'I'm so, so... dispee...' she said, embarrassed that her voice came out quivery.

'Oh no, you are upset. Please do not worry yourself. Here let's gather everything up and then you are coming to sit with me.'

26

The woman's kindness was Annie's undoing. Tears spilled over and ran down her cheeks. She couldn't look up. Instead she carried on searching for the errant oranges. Before she could lie down to check under the cabinets, an arm reached towards her and gently tugged her to her feet.

'Do not worry yourself about the floor. It is nothing to be sad about. I am Carlotta of the shop's name and I do not mind about the mess.'

Carlotta called out in Italian and a teenage girl emerged from a back room. A rapid exchange ensued as Annie was propelled gently into a small sitting room and deposited on a low seat.

'Here. Drink this and relax.'

A small cup of dark, rich coffee was thrust into Annie's hands.

'I'm sorry if my brother upset you,' said Carlotta as she lowered herself into a seat next to Annie's. 'Giovanni is not as grumpy as he sometimes seems.'

'It is I who am sorry. I attacked him.'

Carlotta snorted. 'Yes, you did. It was

very funny. I shall be laughing for days. When you hitted him with your head ... He thought you were trying to kill him.'

'Is that what he said?' Annie asked in horror. 'Sì.' Carlotta went off into giggles, which quickly became contagious. Before long they were both helpless with laughter, tears streaming down both of their faces and their sides aching. Annie hadn't laughed so hard in a long time.

'I'm so sorry about the mess,' said Annie, when she'd finally got control of her laughter.

'Don't you mean désolée?' asked Carlotta, setting off a fresh wave of giggles.

When they'd sobered up enough to speak Carlotta asked, 'Are you anything to do with Castello di Giacobbella? I hear this ruin has been bought by an English lady.'

'My Aunt Tilly bought it recently. I have come out here to give her a hand with the renovation,' Annie explained.

'What is she doing to that huge pile of falling — down stones?' Carlotta frowned.

'She wants to turn it into a hotel.'

'A hotel! Are you sure? This is craziness. Why would anyone want to come and be staying in Vescovina for a holiday?'

Annie smiled at Carlotta's expression. Her eyes were comically wide with disbelief.

'It's beautiful,' Annie stated simply.

'Pfft. Vescovina is a crumbly backwater in the middle of no place. There is nothing but vines and olive trees. I would not come here on holiday.'

'But it's so pretty and peaceful,' Annie argued. How could Carlotta not see the beauty all around?

'Pretty and peaceful does not pay for living. Your aunt has wasted her money. No one will want to come here,' said Carlotta adamantly.

Annie adjusted her stubby ponytail. 'Why do you stay here if nothing ever happens?' she asked.

Carlotta shrugged. 'My family have always lived here. I do not wish to be apart from my parents.' They sipped their coffees in silence for a moment. Annie, whose parents had travelled the world for work and were doing so again in retirement, couldn't imagine a family with such a solid base.

'Aunt Tilly doesn't want to turn it into a beach type of holiday hotel,' Annie said eventually. 'She is talking about yoga retreats and that sort of thing. I wouldn't worry about her. She has an uncanny ability of getting ventures exactly right.'

'I suppose that could work.' Carlotta's expression wasn't encouraging. She clearly thought Tilly was mad. 'Is your aunt the lady with the beads in her hair?'

'That's the one,' said Annie.

'Her Italian is very good. She looks kind of … ' Carlotta waved her hand around in the air. 'Floaty. I wouldn't think she was a good business person from the way she looks.'

'Nobody ever does. Perhaps that is why she is so successful. Everyone thinks she's a relaxed, hippy type but she's actually a shark.'

Annie grinned. She'd never discuss it

with anyone but Tilly had made millions over the years. This was the first time she'd bought a castle, though.

'Thank you for the espresso.' She finished the intense drink. 'I should be going.'

'Si, I must return to the shop also. Hopefully Sofia has replaced all your items for you.'

'Oh, there was no need to do that,' said Annie, embarrassed. 'You've been so generous when I caused such a scene.'

'Don't say sorry again. It was so funny. I have not laughed so hard in a long time.'

The two women smiled at the memory of their shared laughter and stood up.

'Your brother was so angry,' Annie commented as they made their way back to the shop.

'Ah,' said Carlotta softly, 'this was not your fault.'

Carlotta appeared to be looking anywhere but at her and in the process she looked just like Molly when she was trying to hide something.

31

'Are you sure?' asked Annie, curious as to what Carlotta could be hiding. Giovanni's anger certainly seemed as if it was directed at her.

Carlotta didn't answer Annie's question as she was rushing over to help Sofia deal with a surprisingly long line of customers. Annie didn't think they'd been in the sitting room that long but the shop had totally changed in character while they'd been gone.

Now, instead of the peaceful haven she'd entered, the shop was frenetic with customers calling to one another and shouts of laughter punctuating dramatic bursts of speech.

Annie spotted her replenished basket behind the counter. She picked it up and wandered around the store adding a few remaining items including some dry shampoo. Although she knew she'd have to wash her hair in the stream at some point, she doubted she was brave enough to do it every day. Dry shampoo was a necessary purchase if she was to stop her hair looking awful for the entire duration of her stay.

By the time she reached the counter Sofia had disappeared and it was just Carlotta dealing with the chattering customers. Annie placed her items on the short conveyor belt and Carlotta began ringing them through.

'Ah, sì, one of the busy woman's essentials,' Carlotta said as she handed over the dry shampoo.

Annie laughed. 'It's also essential for someone who doesn't have access to running water.'

'The castello has no water! But this is terrible. You must come here and use my shower.'

'Oh no, I couldn't possibly,' said Annie, embarrassed yet hoping Carlotta would see through her protest and insist. The thought of warm, running water was enticing. Enticing enough to get over her typically British embarrassment if pressed.

Fortunately Carlotta ignored her response. 'Yes, you must come. I have a good idea. You must come tomorrow evening. I will make us a dinner. You can use my shower and we can also have some wine.'

'That sounds blissful,' said Annie, deciding not to protest again in case the delicious prospect was whisked away from her.

'I close the shop at six. You are welcome to come any time after that. And bring your Zia Tilly. It would be good to speak to this crazy lady.'

Annie laughed. Crazy was probably a good description of Tilly. Although entrepreneurial and brave were also fitting epithets.

'Thanks. I'll look forward to it.'

As she said it, Annie realised that she meant it. In Carlotta she recognised a sense of comradeship; the feeling that, given enough time, they could become good friends.

Now if they could just get the electricity working back at the castle, life on Isola di Cigni would be perfect.

3

Giovanni paused in his sister's court-yard. The smell of her cooking drifted down to him and he took a deep appreciative breath. You could always rely on Carlotta to produce mouthwateringly good food and after a long, hard day he really needed the comfort of a delicious meal.

He bounded up the steps to her family's apartment above her shop and pushed the front door open without knocking. He found Carlotta at the kitchen stove, stirring a large pot.

'Is there any for me in there?' he asked, kicking off his boots and leaving them by a pile of others near an almost empty shoe rack.

'It depends,' she said without looking up, 'whether you are going to apologise to Annie.'

'Who?' he said, swiping some bread off the table before Carlotta could object.

'The lady at the shop today — the one you growled at.'

'Ah.' He rubbed his chin, which was still sore. 'Do you mean the lady who attacked me?'

Carlotta snorted with laughter. 'She accidentally bumped into you and you bit her head off. You actually accused her of trying to kill you!'

'Well, she really went for it. I'm covered in bruises.' He leaned over to grab some more bread but this time Carlotta was quicker and whipped it away from him.

'Leave some for the rest of us. Go and say hello to your daughter. She's been asking for you every five minutes for the last hour.'

Giovanni didn't need to be told twice. He would much rather spend time with Serena than talk about the English lady who may or may not be the harbinger of doom for Vescovina, but who was definitely too attractive for his peace of mind. He'd only spent a few seconds in her company but her troubled grey eyes had swum into his mind with unwelcome frequency throughout the day. He'd even laughed at her terrible attempt to communicate, once he'd calmed down.

The problem was that no matter how attractive the newcomer was, her arrival must be linked to the goings-on at the castle ruins and that concerned him deeply.

The slog of the day and the worries over the future of his farm fell away as his five-year-old daughter launched herself into his arms.

Holding her tightly, her dark curls tickled his chin as he listened to her prattle on about her day. He sank onto a sofa, still holding her firmly, and wondered, not for the first time, how Serena's mother could live without this. Serena and her lively innocence were a balm to even the hardest-hearted person.

'I'm hungry, Papà,' said Serena eventually. 'Auntie Carlotta is cooking. Let's go and see if it's ready.'

He had to hope Carlotta was joking about him apologising to the English lady before he ate. He didn't know where she was staying, for one thing. She couldn't be staying at the castle. The last time he'd been there, it had been nothing but rubble inside.

'So, are you going to do it?' asked Carlotta as she handed out portions of delicately-cooked pasta and a thick, rich-looking sauce.

'Do what?' he murmured, watching as his daughter promptly covered her face in the sauce.

'Apologise to Annie.'

So that was her name; it suited her somehow. 'Why is it so important to you?' he asked as Carlotta joined him at the table.

'I liked her and she was in tears after you left. You hurt her feelings.'

A twinge of remorse curled in his chest; perhaps he had been a little harsh in his reaction. She hadn't meant to head-butt him after all.

'OK, I'll apologise next time I see her,' he said, twirling pasta around his fork.

'Good, you can do it tomorrow.'

He frowned. 'Why am I going to see her tomorrow?'

'She's coming here to use the shower.'

'What? Why?' asked Giovanni, dropping his fork onto his plate.

Serena giggled at the resultant clatter. Giovanni reached over and tried to wipe some sauce from her face but it seemed to make things worse. Oh well, he'd just have to stick her in the shower when they got home.

'She's camping and doesn't have access to running water. She'll probably be here when you come to pick up Serena,' Carlotta explained.

'She is something to do with the castle, then?' Giovanni said, picking up his fork and gathering up some more pasta.

'She and her aunt are doing it up. They're going to turn it into a hotel apparently.'

'Hmm,' muttered Giovanni darkly.

'You can't dislike her just because her aunt bought the land you wanted. Both women are very friendly. You never know, you might be able to work out a deal with them or something.'

'It isn't just about the castle's lands,' he protested. 'I think there's more to this than a mere renovation of that dilapidated castle.'

'Oh, Giovanni,' said Carlotta, reaching across the table and squeezing his hand. 'You've become so suspicious and un-trusting recently. I know Ashley hurt you badly, but not everyone is like your ex-wife.'

Giovanni glanced across at Serena but she hadn't picked up on the comment about her absent mother. Flecks of sauce were now dotting her dark hair and he groaned inwardly. A shower was one thing, but de-tangling her hair after a wash took ages. There would be no quick bedtime routine this evening.

He turned back to his sister who was regarding him with large, sad eyes. It was a look she was perfecting now that he was a single parent. He pulled his hand free.

'I know not everyone is like Ashley but this isn't about me. It's about the stretch of land between the castle and the beach.

I am sure there are plans to build there and that will destroy the area. Not to mention having a devastating effect on my farm. It's taken years to reach the stage I'm at now and I don't want that to be destroyed by two eccentric British ladies.'

Carlotta leaned back in her chair.

'I think you're wrong. Vescovina isn't a tourist destination. Why would anyone want to build a large hotel complex here?'

Giovanni held up his hand and began to count the reasons off on his fingers.

'The land is cheap, the beach is unspoilt, there is no competition and we have persuadable planning officials in our town council. It's the perfect place to build a hotel. I'm not saying that Annie and her aunt necessarily have anything to do with it but you have to agree it's a convenient coincidence that they've bought the castle right next to that stretch of land. I'm not inclined to trust them until we know more about them.'

'Well,' said Carlotta, picking up her

own fork and turning her attention back to her meal. 'You'll have a chance to ask her after you've apologised tomorrow evening.'

Giovanni sighed softly and began to scrape the remains of the sauce from the edge of his bowl. His own cooking was nowhere near as good as his sister's and he relished the days he could come and eat here.

He didn't want to argue with Carlotta. She was not only his closest ally but she also helped him out whenever he needed someone to look after his daughter, which she did without complaining, even though she had her own business and family to look after.

He changed the subject and asked about his niece, Sofia, who was putting on a show at the local theatre later tonight. Carlotta quickly forgot about Annie as she regaled him with stories of Sofia learning her lines — or not, as it turned out.

It wasn't until much later, when Serena was joyfully splashing him with water as he tried to wash the sauce out of her hair, that Giovanni thought more ab out the British lady and her castle. It was strange that Carlotta was so insistent that he apologise to her new friend. If he hadn't known better, he would have sworn she was trying to match-make.

But that was impossible. Carlotta was always scathing of women who threw themselves at him just because he'd once been a model. It had to be for some other reason — he just couldn't fathom what.

4

Tilly twisted her fingers around the straps of her handbag. 'Are you sure you don't mind?'

'Of course not. It sounds like too good an opportunity to miss. Besides, it doesn't really need the two of us here to supervise things. The workmen are doing a great job all by themselves.'

'I don't like the thought of you staying up here all by yourself, though,' said Tilly, looking around anxiously as if expecting a madman to jump out of a bush. 'I wish you'd take up my offer and let me pay for you to stay in a guest house.'

Annie gently squeezed her aunt's arm. She knew she'd be out of her mind with worry if her daughter decided to camp out on her own on a steep hill, but the truth was, they'd not seen another soul up here apart from the builders. They were only ever disturbed by a passing goat. She felt far safer here than in her terraced house in Britain. And she was used to being on her own. 'Don't worry about me. Carlotta's promised to feed me while you're away and I can always stay in her spare room if it comes to it. Look,' said Annie, interrupting her aunt before she could start worrying all over again. 'Here comes your taxi. Let me help you with your suitcase.'

Annie bundled her aunt into the cab and waved cheerfully as the car took her away. She glanced at her watch to confirm what her stomach was telling her — it was time for lunch.

She gathered up an old wallpapering table she'd used before and set it up outside the castle front door. A large white sheet hid the worst of the sticky spills and she set about arranging food she'd bought at Carlotta's earlier that morning. She sliced a loaf of bread and set it in the centre. Around it she arranged the hams, spreads and cheeses she'd bought. At the end of the table she added some of the fruit and soft-looking sponge cake, which she cut into large pieces.

Ben, the burly foreman, emerged from the castle first.

'You've done us proud again,' he said in his thick northern accent.

She smiled. 'How has work gone this morning?'

'Good,' said Ben as he loaded up his plate and launched into a long speech about crank beams and load-bearing walls. Thank goodness he was speaking English because she only understood about half of what was being said. If he'd only spoken Italian, like most of the workers, then she'd have been lost.

'Plumber's coming this afternoon,' said Ben when he'd finished relating what they'd been up to this morning. 'He'll want to talk to you about your idea for a rooftop pool.'

'Does he speak English?'

'He does but I can translate if there are any problems. Your Italian is coming on a treat, though. You'll be better than me in no time and I've been out here eleven years now.'

Annie laughed.

'I don't think so, but thank you for the compliment. When will the plumber arrive?'

'He'll be here when the boys knock off. Around four, I should think.'

'Do you need me for anything this afternoon?'

'I don't think so. We'll crack on with what we started this morning. Has Tilly gone?'

'Yes, she didn't want to leave me but another hotel coming up for sale on the other side of the island is too good an opportunity to miss. It's at such a bargain price and I'm sure that Tilly can work her magic on it if she manages to buy it. Although I'll miss her, I'm glad she's gone in a way. There isn't enough work for the two of us and I was starting to feel like a spare wheel.'

Ben look outraged.

'You've done wonders in the few days you've been here. Your aunt has an excellent head for business but anyone can see that you've got the more sympathetic eye for what looks good. The lads and I all agree.'

Annie felt herself turn pink with pleasure. She'd not done a great deal with her career prospects, preferring to put Molly first, so to hear she was good at something filled her with joy.

'What are those ruins?' she asked, pointing to the crumbling bricks she could see in the distance, which had been intriguing her since she'd first arrived.

'Those are the remains of a Roman villa. It's quite extensive but not really maintained. Maybe it would have been if this was more of a tourist island, but as it is, it's been left to gently decay.'

'Is it worth going to see them?' asked Annie, who was going regardless but didn't want to be disappointed if they weren't up to much.

'Oh yes, they're definitely worth a visit. They are built on such a lovely spot, too. It's very tranquil down there. Unless, that is, you believe the local legend.'

'What legend?' asked Annie.

'They're said to be haunted by a young

boy and his dog.'

'That doesn't sound too scary,' said Annie. 'I've met lots of young boys and they can be a bit smelly and go on about computer games a little too much, but I've never found them frightening.'

Ben laughed. 'That sounds like a fairly accurate description of my two sons so I know what you mean. But some of the older generation are really terrified and won't go down there around dusk. My neighbour won't go there at all.'

'I thought I might go and see them this afternoon if you really don't need me.'

'Aye, you'll enjoy that and no, we don't need you until four. Mind you follow the path, now. I don't want to have to send down a search party.'

She laughed and promising that she would, left him to the rest of his lunch break while she went to dig out a pair of trainers.

She collected a crusty roll from her hamper and then pulled some of the delicious mortadella ham and creamy cheese she'd discovered yesterday out of the small fridge Ben had loaned them. It was powered by an ancient-looking generator that rumbled noisily. She'd be glad to get away from it for an hour or so. She added a few fruits to her rough picnic, anxious to get going.

Setting off towards the ruins, she realised she couldn't follow a direct route to them. The way was too heavily blocked by thick weeds. She spotted a rough path cut through some tall pine trees. The trees were a little way off from the castle, but the track seemed to be heading in the right direction and she'd promised Ben she'd follow the path. She could always turn back if she was wrong.

Dried, spiky pine needles crunched underfoot as she stepped into the shade of the trees. In places, thorny weeds almost cut the path in two and she stepped gingerly around them. The wind rustled branches above her but all else was silent.

At one point the trail swerved right, away from the direction of the ruins.

Annie stopped. Should she strike off the path, through the trees, or carry on? She settled for staying on the trail; it would be embarrassing if Ben did have to send out a search party. She was rewarded for following the path by it swinging sharply to the left not long afterwards. Eventually the trees petered out and the first remnants of an ancient wall emerged from the undergrowth.

Annie stopped to look at it, trying to imagine what it could have been; part of a house or a roadway? There was no way of knowing, no matter which angle she looked at the stones from. Perhaps they were just part of an old wall. She started to tingle with excitement.

She'd devoured many books on the Roman Empire at school and they'd captured her imagination. As she followed the stones of the ruins, she imagined a rich senator walking the same steps with his wife or perhaps his lover. Had they been happy living here with such beautiful views or had their lives been short and brutal?

Everything was still, bar a distant tweeting of a bird. The sun beat down from a cloudless sky. Annie rested on a low wall and pulled out the food from her bag. She pulled apart the bread with her fingers and stuffed the opening full of the cuts of ham and cheese. She added some tomatoes and then bit ravenously into the sandwich. Her mind wandered, flitting between her ideas for the hotel and worrying about what Molly was up to.

A flash of black caught her attention and brought her back to her surroundings. She turned, but there was nothing to see except for the tumbling ruins and the piercing blue sky.

The sound of a child's giggle floated through the air. Annie stood and tiptoed in the direction of the movement she thought she'd seen.

Another giggle sounded, much closer.

Heart pounding, she rounded another corner. This time there was no mistaking the sight of a small child crossing the path in front of her and disappearing behind a tall stone wall. She stood still, waiting. Suddenly the air was pierced by a high-pitched screech.

For a moment Annie stood frozen in terror. Was this really the ghost of Ben's legend? Then she was running towards the sound, her maternal instinct to protect kicking in.

She rounded a corner and smacked straight into a hard body.

In shock, she leapt backwards and stumbled over a sharp rock. Warm hands reached out and grabbed her before she could fall to the ground.

'You again,' rumbled a deep voice above her. She looked up. It was the man she'd assaulted in Carlotta's. Giovanni. His blue eyes, so like his sister's, were staring down at her.

'What are you doing here?' she demanded, the shock of the last few minutes robbing her of her politeness.

'I'm playing with Serena, my daughter. What are you doing here?'

'Papà?' said a small voice from behind them.

Annie turned to see a pre-school child looking uncertainly between Giovanni and herself. Serena was dressed in a black dress dotted with pink flowers. A riot of dark curls fell over her shoulders. It was ridiculous that even for a split second, she had mistaken this little girl for a ghost.

'Well?' demanded Giovanni as Serena slid past Annie and climbed into his arms.

'I ... ' Annie froze. For some reason she felt inexplicably guilty. As if she'd been caught doing something naughty.

She straightened. What business was it of his? They weren't on private land. She'd done nothing wrong. OK, so she'd hit him quite hard yesterday but most people would see the funny side.

'I'm exploring,' she said, more calmly than she was feeling. 'I'm sorry I bumped into you again. I hope you weren't hurt this time.'

She turned to go. The sooner she was away from this strange man, the better.

'Why were you running so fast?'

Annie turned back. Serena was peering at her from her father's shoulder. When she caught Annie looking at her, she hid her face in Giovanni's shirt. Annie smiled; she remembered Molly doing the same when confronted by a stranger. She could still feel the weight of her daughter in her arms, even though it had been many years since she'd been able to pick her up.

'I thought I heard a child in danger,' she said. 'I wanted to make sure everything was all right.'

Was his hard stare softening? 'You're a mother,' he stated.

Although it wasn't a question, Annie answered, 'Yes, I have a daughter.'

She hadn't imagined it. His stance was more relaxed and he was almost smiling.

Giovanni nodded. 'How is she finding life in Italy? There cannot be much in the way of luxury up at the castle.'

'Oh,' she said surprised. 'She's not in Italy.

She's in Britain. She's — '

Everything about Giovanni tightened and the glower returned full force. He muttered something darkly in Italian and then turned and walked away. Annie stood rooted to the spot. What had happened there? What on earth could she have said to make him react in such a way? And how could such a lovely lady like Carlotta have such a grumpy brother?

She glanced at her watch. She needed to start heading back to the castle now for her meeting with the plumber — but there was still most of the ruins left to explore. She would come back tomorrow. Hopefully without a grumpy man disturbing her solitude.

5

Annie stood under the spray of Carlotta's shower and closed her eyes. Showers were a luxury she'd never appreciated before the alternative was washing in an icy-cold stream.

After a few seconds of allowing the warm water to run over her, she began to scrub herself clean. She didn't want to abuse her new friend's hospitality.

She took her time getting dry. Carlotta had been looking after her young niece this evening when Annie had arrived earlier and, coward that she was, she didn't want to bump into Giovanni when he came to pick her up.

Once dressed, she opened the door a crack and listened. The apartment was quiet. She must have missed Giovanni's arrival and departure, thank goodness. She pulled the door fully open and made her way back to the kitchen.

She gasped in surprise when she

found Carlotta and Giovanni glaring at one another in silence.

Before any of the adults could speak, Serena arrived carrying an empty rucksack and armfuls of toys, scattering them as she moved. Unaware of the mood in the kitchen, she chatted away.

Giovanni bent to kiss his daughter swiftly on the top of her head. Ignoring Annie, he began speaking to his sister in Italian.

Annie began to pick up the fallen belongings as a rapid conversation took place. Normally people spoke English or slow Italian in front of her and she could pick up the gist of a conversation, but this was way too fast. She had a feeling they were arguing about her, but couldn't fathom why.

She put the collected toys on a nearby table and smiled at Serena, who gazed shyly back. The little girl was quite taken with Annie, especially after Carlotta had told her the story of Annie hitting her father while doing her shopping.

'Thanks,' said Giovanni gruffly. He

stuffed the toys back into Serena's rucksack and then with a terse, 'Grazie,' to
his sister and a final glare for her he left.

'What on earth have I done to upset
your brother?' asked Annie. 'It can't
possibly be because I accidentally hit
him with a basket.'

Carlotta sighed and shook her head.

'You have done nothing. But... Please
sit and I will tell you everything.'

★ ★ ★

'So let me get this straight,' said Annie,
taking another sip of deliciously cold
wine. 'Your brother thinks I'm some sort
of hotel mastermind intent on taking
over the island and turning it into Costa
del Nightmare.'

''Del' is Spanish,' said Carlotta, grinning. Annie smiled in response but didn't
comment.

She was glad her language incompe-
tence was providing some amusement,
but she really ought to learn some Italian properly if she was going to stay out

here for six months. She twirled her hair around her fingers. Carlotta's explanation didn't really make sense.

'I don't understand why Giovanni believes we are going to clear the scrubland below the hotel and build a large complex there. It would ruin the views from the castle and I don't think that land is even connected to us. I'll find out, but please reassure him that we have no plans to do so.'

'You must look into who does own that land. There are rumours that someone plans to build a big hotel there, and it's not just my paranoid brother who thinks it's true. If not you, who?'

Annie's stomach tightened. A large hotel complex built in the scrubland near the castello would not only destroy the view, but also ruin any hopes of the place becoming a quiet retreat.

'Surely no one could build there,' she argued. 'It's so close to the Roman ruins it could spoil them completely.'

'It will spoil the whole area,' Carlotta agreed, 'but the council can ignore any objections.'

'Surely not!'

'It's a common problem. Only last year a rich landowner from the mainland built a monstrosity of a house a little further along the coast. Everyone was up in arms because it's quite different from the original stonework you see everywhere else around here but in the end there was nothing we could do to stop it.'

'How will I find out if the rumours are true?' Anxiety turned the wine to acid in Annie's stomach.

Carlotta tilted her head. 'You could ask the council, but they are not always truthful.'

'How did your brother find out about this?'

'When he tried to buy the castello, he — '

'Giovanni tried to buy Aunt Tilly's castle? No wonder he's been so angry with me.'

'I really don't think he's angry with you. It is, well, I think things are tough for him at the moment. We must make allowances.'

Carlotta pulled a face which suggested she might find this a difficult thing to do.

Annie found it hard to imagine the gorgeous Giovanni, with his beautiful daughter and presumably equally stunning wife, having a difficult time of it but maybe she wasn't seeing the bigger picture. She of all people knew you shouldn't judge people by how their lives looked from the outside. Anyone looking at her would assume she was a middle-aged single woman, not a widow with a grown-up daughter.

'What did he want with the castle?' Annie asked, twirling linguine around her fork.

She managed to get the forkful of pasta into her mouth without it dribbling down her chin and was impressed with herself. When she'd started this meal of linguine with traditional local sausages, she'd been a calamity with the long pasta. Carlotta had taught her how to expertly gather up the pasta so it stuck to the fork. After a few attempts she was becoming quite the expert.

'It wasn't the castle he was after. He wanted the land that came with it to extend his farm.'

'He has a *farm*?'

Giovanni looked ab out as far away from a farmer as Annie could possibly imagine. She would have been less astounded if Carlotta had announced he was an underwear model.

'Yes,' said Carlotta, her lips twitching. 'Why is that so surprising?'

Annie laughed. 'I thought I hid my reaction quite well.'

'You have a very...' Carlotta waved her hands around as she searched for the right word and Annie renewed her vow to learn Italian. 'Your face always shows what you are feeling,' continued her friend. 'It's one of the things I really like about you. Here, have some more wine.'

Annie mulled this statement over. She hoped she wasn't as easy to read as Carlotta suggested because if so, Giovanni would know exactly what she thought of him.

As Carlotta filled her glass, she tried to think of a reason she was surprised about her brother's chosen career which didn't sound insulting. She settled on, 'He doesn't dress like a farmer.'

She hadn't given his clothes much thought before this evening but casting her mind back, he was always dressed in jeans and a T-shirt. She would prefer not to notice how the T-shirts defined his muscular arms, but she couldn't deny that she had. He was an attractive man. She just wished he wasn't so horrible to her all the time.

'Are you imagining that all Italian farmers dress like peasants?' asked Carlotta, amused.

'No,' protested Annie, although that was exactly what she'd been thinking. 'What does he farm?' she asked, quickly changing the subject.

'Olives mainly but limone, limes, pomodori, that's tomatoes. He doesn't have animals.'

'Is there any other land he can buy?' Annie asked, finishing her linguine and scraping up the delicious sauce.

Carlotta shrugged. 'The land that came with the castello was the best. It runs alongside his farm. I don't know what he will do now, but ... It is the least of his problems right at the moment.'

Not wanting to be nosy but also desperately wanting to find out what could possibly be wrong in Giovanni's life Annie asked, as casually as she could manage, 'What is wrong with Giovanni?'

'I've promised my brother I won't discuss his private life until he is willing for it to become known to everyone. Even though I trust you not to go around spreading gossip, it's best I keep my promise. You know what brothers are like?'

'Mmm,' she murmured non-committally.

'Do you have any brothers?' asked Carlotta, topping up their wine glasses again.

'No, I'm an only child. My parents travelled a lot with my dad's job so I mostly grew up with my aunt, who's single.'

The conversation moved on from Giovanni and an hour later Annie realised it was time to head back to the tent. The sun had set some time ago. 'I should go,' she said, unfurling herself from the sofa and stretching. 'Thank you so much for this evening. It's been lovely.'

'Thank you for coming,' said Carlotta. 'It has been good getting to know you more. You must come again for a shower and stay for dinner.'

'Yes, please,' said Annie, still feeling the benefits of those ten minutes under hot water.

'I have to take Sofia to il teatro tomorrow — she is singing in a show. Please say you'll come the day after.'

'I'd love to,' said Annie, sliding into her shoes. 'Can I bring anything?'

'No, grazie. I enjoy cooking and your liking of my food has been very good for me. I will cook for us again and I will invite my friend, Greta. She used to teach Italian to English people. Perhaps she can help you to learn our language.'

'Oh, yes. It would be great to stop making a fool of myself by saying the wrong words.'

Carlotta snorted and the two women hugged goodbye.

The walk back to her tent was surprisingly easy. Either she was getting used to the climb or two glasses of wine was the optimum amount to help. Her torchlight bounced over the lumpy path and the cool evening air kissed her cheeks. She'd be very upset if she found out that Molly was wandering around the countryside in the dark like this, but she felt entirely safe.

Her thoughts turned back to Giovanni and his suspicions about the hotel being built on the scrubland next to the castle. It couldn't be true. Something like that would surely have been flagged up to Tilly when she bought the castle. She was pretty certain that was the case in English law — but here, perhaps it wasn't.

First thing tomorrow she needed to find out if the rumour was true. If it was, then it could spell disaster for Tilly's castle.

6

Greta was a very short, thin woman with tight curls and a dirty laugh. Annie liked her immediately and as soon as she finished showering, the two women sat at Carlotta's kitchen table. Some very basic Italian words written on cards were spread before them.

The work surfaces were covered in chopped herbs. Carlotta hadn't yet joined them. Annie could hear her speaking rapid Italian in another room.

'Put these cards into three piles,' said Greta in her perfect English. 'One for words you already know, another for words you think you could guess at and one for the words you haven't got a clue about.'

The already known pile was very small. Greta picked them up.

'I see you know how to greet people,' she said, flicking through the words. 'How much did you know before you came out here?'

'Absolutely nothing,' confessed Annie.

'Then you've picked up quite a bit already. We'll have you speaking like a native in no time at all.'

Annie grinned. 'You're very kind, but … '

'I am never kind,' said Greta and cackled her slightly mad laugh. 'Now I'm going to switch to Italian, using some of the words you know and hopefully you will pick up my meaning.'

Annie frowned in concentration as Greta spoke to her in a slow, steady voice. Because of Greta's elaborate hand gestures she found she could follow most of it.

Greta moved on to showing Annie a handful of cards and asking her to translate them.

'I hope she is not working you too hard, Annie,' said Carlotta, coming into the room carrying her niece. 'Tell her to stop if she becomes too much.'

'I'm enjoying it.' Annie leaned her elbows on the table. 'I know that one,' she said pointing to the card Greta was holding. 'It means

I'm sorry.' 'She's a natural,' said Greta, looking pleased.

'You'll be speaking Italian fluently in no time.'

Annie laughed delightedly. It was great to find something she was good at.

'I hope you like fish, Annie,' said Carlotta, putting Serena down. 'I didn't think to ask last time you were here.'

'There's no food I don't like.' Annie smiled at Serena who was hiding behind her aunt's legs. 'Buongiorno,' she said to the little girl.

Serena burst into giggles.

'You wished her good day,' explained Greta, grinning down at the laughing girl. 'You mean buonasera, which is good evening.'

The girl's laughter was infectious and soon all three grown-ups were laughing too.

'I think that is enough Italian practice for today. I've brought this book for you to borrow. Work your way through chapter one and we'll speak again in two days to see how you are getting on.'

Annie took the battered book from Greta and flicked through it. Its pages were soft and crinkled. 'It's been used many times before by my other students. It's never failed me yet,' said Greta, gathering up the cards.

'Thank you,' said Annie, slipping it into her handbag. 'How would you like me to pay you?'

'Don't worry about paying her,' said Carlotta, waving a spoon. 'She is married to the richest man on the island. She doesn't need your money.'

Greta cackled. 'This is true. Piero is very rich and I do not need to work any more. I'll teach you for the enjoyment of it. Carlotta, is your brother coming to pick up Serena soon?'

Carlotta glanced at the clock.

'He is coming in ten minutes but remember, you are a married woman and you are keeping your hands to yourself.'

'I'll keep my hands to myself but I can't promise not to look. He's gorgeous, isn't he, Annie?'

'Um, well. He's OK, I guess.'

'Mamma mia, only OK! He was a model for several years, wasn't he, Carlotta?'

Ah, so he had been a model. That seemed more realistic than farmer.

'Half the islanders are in love with him,' continued Greta. 'Well, it's probably more than half. I'm only counting the women but I expect lots of the men are, too. I mean, those eyes ... ' Greta stared dreamily into space. Annie glanced at Carlotta, whose blue eyes, so like her brother's, were smiling at her friend's vacant expression. 'Well?' said Greta. 'What do you really think, Annie?'

'I've noticed he does indeed have eyes.' Carlotta laughed. 'I'm glad you're not throwing yourself at him, Annie. I had enough of girls and their — how do you say? — silliness all the time when he is around. They look just like that.'

Carlotta pointed her spoon at Greta.

Annie laughed and Greta grinned unrepentantly. 'Did you find out any more about the development Giovanni thinks might take place on the land near the castle?' Annie asked, changing the subject. She didn't want to talk about Giovanni himself. It would be just her luck to opine that he looked handsome but was too moody for her, just as he walked through the door. She didn't like being the subject of his fierce glares.

'What development is this?' Greta asked.

Annie explained about the potential large development being built on the coast adding, 'I've tried to find out if the rumours are true but no one on the council will speak to me. I got Ben, the foreman, to ring up to try in Italian but we were blocked at every turn. Surely they would tell me if there wasn't going to be a development. This evasiveness is making me feel uneasy.'

Greta pulled a face. 'No one is going to like a large hotel there.'

'Not even if it brings in lots of jobs for locals?' asked Annie.

'Not even then. It is a special part of

the island. We locals like to go to sit on the beach and this is one of the best ones for not being overrun with tourists as is happening in other towns.'

Annie felt a small knot of worry, which had been lodged in her stomach since she'd heard the news two days ago, slightly unwind. If the locals were against the build, then surely the council couldn't allow it to go ahead. She buried the thought deep down. Hopefully everyone who'd mentioned it was exaggerating.

Serena had come to stand close to her as the adults were talking. Annie tore a sheet of paper from her notepad and slowly folded it in different directions. When she was done, she held it out.

'It's a swan,' she said. 'Cigno.' She pulled down on the tail and the wings flapped.

Serena's eyes lit up. Carefully she took the paper bird from Annie to try the wings herself. Her look of wonder as she made them move made Annie's heart ache. It seemed like only yesterday that Molly was impressed by cleverly folded paper.

'It's for you,' Annie said when Serena tried to hand it back.

Carlotta translated and Serena looked as if Annie had handed her a plate of gold. She carried the swan over to her other toys in the corner of the room and started to introduce them.

'Can I help you make dinner?' asked Annie, tearing her eyes away from the adorable scene. It would not do for her to get broody. She and Hugo had wanted a large family but it wasn't to be. She'd long since resigned herself to the fact, but that didn't stop her longing for more every now and again. Sometimes the feeling was so intense it blindsided her at unexpected moments.

'Thank you but the meal's almost ready,' said Carlotta. 'It really is very simple — a good piece of fish and some herbs. You must sit, relax. Tell us how things are going on up at the castello.'

Annie sat back in the chair and chatted happily about how things had gone for the last few days and what her plans were for the future.

'Wow, a rooftop pool will be paradise,' commented Greta, when Annie told them of her most ambitious idea. 'I would pay good money to visit that myself.'

'And don't forget that she has lots,' said Carlotta, sliding a fillet of fish onto a plate.

'Papà!' cried Serena.

Annie turned to find Giovanni standing in the kitchen doorway. Greta was flicking her hair and smiling at him winningly but he only had eyes for his little girl. She ran to him and he picked her up.

Serena held onto him like a monkey for a moment and then she wriggled free.

Giovanni smiled at his sister and nodded to the two other women but before he could say anything Serena was back, holding her paper swan and chattering about it. She showed him how to make the wings flap and then evidently expected him to do the same as she passed it to him.

76

The fragile piece of paper looked tiny in his massive hands as he obliged his daughter. Although Annie couldn't understand what was being said between them, it was obvious Serena was delighted with her paper present.

She felt a tinge of satisfaction as Giovanni thanked her for making the origami for his daughter. Then she lost the thread of the conversation as he spoke to his sister. Greta continued to smile and pout and flick her hair in his direction but apart from the occasional polite aside, Giovanni kept his attention on his sister.

Annie liked him a little more for it. Another man might not have been able to resist the heavy flirtation from an attractive woman but Giovanni was obviously faithful to his wife.

He left soon after without saying goodbye to Annie. She didn't mind. Serena beamed at her from her father's shoulders and that was enough. Greta sighed as the door closed behind Giovanni. 'That was a waste of some of my best flirtatious looks,' she said. 'I didn't even get a smile in response. Did he not see my artful hair flicking?'

Annie giggled, unable to take Greta seriously. 'You are silly,' said Carlotta. 'It is not worth losing your wealthy husband for a smile from my brother.' She placed dishes of grilled swordfish in front of her guests.

'Piero isn't the jealous type. Plus, I'm sure he'd be more than happy to get a smile from Ashley.'

'Who's Ashley?' asked Annie.

'Giovanni's equally gorgeous wife. She's an American model. Isn't that right, Carlotta? They met on some fashion shoot in somewhere glamorous. Where was it again?'

'It was in Monte Carlo,' said Carlotta.

'I haven't seen her around for a while,' said Greta. 'Is she off somewhere else glamorous? I hadn't realised she'd started working again.'

'Yes, she is working. Now who would like vegetables with this? They are all grown locally.'

'What job is she on?' asked Greta.

'I really don't know,' said Carlotta, not looking at her friend. 'I am not keeping up with what Ashley is up to. Now, shall I pour some wine?'

'Oooh, yes,' said Annie. 'Shall I fetch some?' She made her way to the fridge. It was wrong but she was insanely curious as to why Carlotta, one of the friendliest people she'd met, didn't appear keen on her brother's wife.

★ ★ ★

Giovanni felt his daughter's head finally go limp against his arm and gently he slipped away from her, laying her head on her pillow as he did so.

He watched her sleep and his heart contracted with love. How could her mother miss these precious moments? Before long Serena would be grown and Ashley would have missed it all.

He ran his hand through his hair. Now that Serena was finally asleep, he needed to get on with some paperwork.

Folders were spilling across his desk. Gone were the days of keeping things tidy. He only had to open a file for Serena to come running in to show him something important. Today it had been a worm she'd insisted he return to the mud.

He opened the top folder from the pile, but the lines of figures danced in front of his eyes until he pushed the spreadsheet away.

Carlotta was cross with him. Specifically, she was cross with him for being rude to her new British friend with the big grey eyes that flashed with fire when they looked at him and something akin to adoration when she looked at his daughter.

She was a puzzle. Carlotta swore she was nothing to do with the rumoured big hotel and he was beginning to believe she was right. Work was progressing apace up at the castle, and no one would invest that sort of money if they were going to build a monstrosity right in front of it. But he wasn't going to trust his instinct before he had concrete proof she wasn't involved.

The other thing that truly puzzled him was her reaction to his daughter. She clearly adored Serena and, from Serena's gushing commentary on the swan lady, the feeling appeared to be entirely mutual. So why, then, had Annie left her own daughter in Britain? Didn't she realise that a young child needed their mother?

It was this selfishness which kept him from indulging in looking into those beautiful eyes for too long, or from studying that long, graceful neck. He had enough on his plate without falling under the spell of another heart-breaker.

7

When she wasn't talking to Ben about the progress being made at the castle or poring over the books Tilly had left on property development, Annie was busy learning Italian with Greta or eating long meals with her and Carlotta. She tested her newly-acquired linguistic skills whenever there was a chance to talk to the builders. Occasionally they laughed at her attempts but they seemed pleased to see her trying and would help with her pronunciation.

At the end of two weeks she was able to have a basic conversation, and was proud of herself. At this rate she'd be fluent by the time she returned to Britain — another skill she could add to her growing CV.

'Piove,' she said to Ben when she found him one morning knocking through a wall.

'Is it?' He turned to a nearby window.

'No, it's not raining, although the air feels damp. I was just practising,' she explained.

'The weather is going to turn soon. October's always lovely but now we're nearing November, the weather will turn,' said Ben, bending down and scooping some rubble up in his gloved hands. Annie had ceased to be amazed at the strength of the men who were working on the castle. It seemed stones the size of boulders didn't bother them at all. Ben threw his armful of rubble into a sack on the floor.

'Will it get cold?' asked Annie, who was finding it hard to get warm in the tent now.

'Much cooler. Not as cold and wet as a British winter, but definitely not something you can get through living under canvas.'

'Oh,' said Annie, looking around at the rubble-strewn floor. Although great strides had been made, the castle wasn't anywhere near habitable. 'The offer to stay with Martina and me for a while still stands,' said Ben, referring to an offer he and his wife kept making but which she kept turning down.

'That's very kind of you both,' said Annie. 'I'll speak to Tilly when she gets back later and see what she has planned.'

She really liked Ben and his wife but having been to their apartment and seen how small it was, she knew that they would be making a big sacrifice in having her stay with them.

They had their morning briefing while Ben carried on working. When they'd first begun to work together they'd sat down for about an hour every day but Annie had noticed that after ten minutes of talking, Ben's knees had started to jig up and down and he'd found it hard to concentrate. He'd confessed that sitting down felt like a waste of time when he could be getting on. So now they talked as he worked and Annie made notes. She, too, found it easier to think of ideas if she was moving around.

Twenty minutes later she was wandering back outside with a list of contractors to chase and a handful of logistical problems to work through. She didn't notice the person sitting outside her tent until she almost tripped over him.

'Giovanni,' she said in surprise as he stood, brushing dried mud off his jeans.

'I've been hoping to bump into you — not literally, of course. I remember how hard your head is.' He rubbed his chin. 'I haven't seen you around town for a while so I thought I'd come here instead.'

'What can I do for you?' asked Annie, refusing to rise to the bait. She couldn't believe he was still going on about that first meeting weeks ago.

'Carlotta tells me that you are not planning to develop the area around the castle.'

His gaze was suspicious as if he didn't trust what she'd told his sister — even though she'd been out here for nearly three weeks and hadn't so much as set foot on the scrubland.

'That's right. It doesn't belong to the castle and even if it did, we wouldn't consider building there. It would ruin the whole area. In fact, I don't know where you got the information that someone wants to build there. I've been to the council and I've been told there are no development plans.'

Giovanni nodded. 'They are not always truthful,' he said.

They stared at each other for a moment.

Giovanni handed her an A4 envelope.

'Here is a copy of everything I have collected about the possible development. If it goes ahead it will affect you the most — although it won't be good for me either as your nearest neighbour.'

Annie took the envelope but didn't open it. She didn't know what to say.

He nodded again and then made to walk off. 'Are you still interested in the land that came with the castle?' she asked to his back.

'Why are you asking?' he said, turning slowly. Good grief, he was frustrating. Surely it was obvious. She wasn't about to taunt him that he couldn't have it.

'I've spoken to Tilly,' Annie said.

'While we want some of the land for our guests to move about in, we don't need it all. If you still want to buy some, perhaps we can come to an arrangement.'

'Thank you,' said Giovanni. 'I would be very interested. If you have time now, we could walk to where our land meets and I can show you how much I would like to purchase.'

Annie did have time, but she wasn't keen on spending any more of it with Giovanni than she absolutely had to.

'Tilly will be back later. It might be better to talk to her,' she suggested.

'I'm not available later. Come, let's do it now.' Giovanni set off, heading inland away from the sea and any area Annie had explored so far. She hurried to keep up with his long strides.

'Carlotta tells me you are still camping,' he commented after a while.

'Yes,' said Annie. 'It's a beautiful spot.'

'It will soon be too cold for you to stay in a tent. I have a cottage on the edge of the farm, not far from the castle. We will walk near it today. I'll show you. You could stay there if you wished.' Annie was stunned. She had not expected an offer like this from a man she was sure didn't like her — even though he now knew her to be innocent of trying to develop the scrubland. 'Thank you, that's a kind offer,' she said.

She would much prefer to live alone rather than under Ben's family's feet — even if it did make her indebted to Giovanni.

'Carlotta suggested it,' said Giovanni gruffly.

They walked in silence for another five minutes until they came to a rough gravel road.

'This is where the castello's land ends,' he said, tapping his foot on the dried grass. 'My land starts there.'

On the far side of the track a long, green hedge ran along the edge until it disappeared around a corner. Behind the hedge Annie could just make out the gnarled wood of many olive trees. From what she could see, the farm looked well-maintained and prosperous.

They turned and looked back up the hill. Annie could just make out the top of the castle, poking out from the surrounding vegetation.

'I would be interested in buying the land from here,' he said, indicating the ground beneath their feet, 'as far as that line of trees.'

It was a sizeable area, and the sale would bring in a good chunk of capital. Losing it wouldn't detract from the grounds of the hotel, either.

'OK,' she said. 'I'll speak to Tilly later but I can't see a problem with that. It's one thing less to think about. Although I should check that you're planning not to build on the land?'

Giovanni gave an unexpected bark of laughter. The amusement in his face softened his features. 'I deserved that,' he said. 'No, I can promise you I will not build on the land. I'd like to grow more fruit trees. Come, it's not far to the cottage.' Annie followed him to the bend in the road.

They came across a grey, square

building that was not in the slightest bit romantic or in keeping with the other buildings Annie had seen on the island. It certainly didn't fit her notion of a cottage.

'It's not very pretty,' Giovanni commented, 'but it's functional and it has running water, which I'm told you're lacking at the moment.'

Inside was a basic living area with a small kitchen at one end and utilitarian seating.

'There are two bedrooms, so your aunt can stay too,' said Giovanni. 'The bathroom's there.'

Annie stepped into the miniscule but very clean bathroom. To her relief, there was a shower. She'd just about be able to squeeze into it but it was better than washing in the stream, which was now nearly intolerable. It was also more convenient than trekking to Carlotta's apartment.

She stepped back into the central room.

'You don't have to stay here if it's

too small,' said Giovanni, his shoulders hunched.

'Thanks, it's perfect. How much do you want for the rent?' she asked as she pulled open the fridge. It was sparkling clean, empty and blessedly silent, unlike the generator that powered the tiny one she was using at the moment.

Giovanni cleared his throat. 'I don't need any money for it. It will be good to have it occupied.'

Before she could thank him, he went outside.

Annie really couldn't work him out. To let her and Tilly stay here for free was so generous but he was still so unfriendly. What was his problem?

8

'It's a bit tenuous,' said Tilly. The documents Giovanni had given Annie about the supposed development lay on the table before them.

'I don't know,' said Annie, picking up what she thought was the most incriminating bit of evidence. 'As much as I'd like to believe it's not true, I think there could be something in this.'

Tilly took a sip of tea and leaned back in her chair. They'd been lucky that Giovanni had offered them the use of his cottage. No sooner had Tilly returned this afternoon than the heavens had opened, and staying in the tent had ceased to be an option. The rain still hammered against the windows but now they were under a solid roof Annie found the sound comfortingly familiar.

'Tell me what it is ab out this picture that convinces you Giovanni's right about this development,' said Tilly.

'It's this print-out from the Global Hotel website. Their announcement about the upcoming hotel isn't specific about location but I'm sure these photos show the coastline near here.'

Tilly took the print-out from Annie and held it up to the light of the small lamp next to her.

'It could be any coastline in the Med,' she concluded after a moment's study.

'See this point here, and this.' Annie indicated parts of the photo. 'They look to me like distinctive parts of the coastline below the castle.'

Tilly squinted. 'How can you be so sure?'

'Without TV there hasn't been a great deal for me to do in the evenings other than gaze out to sea,' said Annie ruefully.

There was no doubt in her mind that this was a photo taken of the coast below. Whether that was because it was an attractive piece of land and therefore good for promotional purposes or whether it was because this was the planned site of their next hotel was anyone's guess.

'What other evidence is there?' asked Tilly. 'There's this letter to Giovanni explaining why his application to buy the land has been turned down. It seems to imply that a hotel complex is going to be built and extended farmland won't be in keeping with the new development.' Annie slid the piece of paper towards her aunt.

'This is Giovanni's English translation though, isn't it?' queried Tilly.

'What are you implying?' asked Annie.

'He believes in this potential development even though there's a lack of any solid evidence. I'm not suggesting he's lying to us but maybe he's slanted his translation to emphasise the development. Maybe the original letter referred to my plans for the castle and he misconstrued it.'

'Hmm, it's possible but somehow I doubt it. Giovanni appears to be a very black or white person and his English is flawless. I believe that this is a direct translation — but if it makes you feel better I'll check with Greta when I see her.'

'Well, I don't know this Giovanni at all,' said Tilly. 'But from what you've told me of your encounters he seems slightly odd, although I can't fault his generosity in letting us stay here for free. I think we should take this whole development thing with a very large pinch of salt.'

'Hmm,' said Annie again as she gathered up the papers and slid them back into the envelope. 'Maybe I've misrepresented Giovanni. He's been grumpy to me but he doesn't come across as delusional. I'll look into it some more. We don't want to wake up one morning to find a monstrous hotel blocking the castle's view of the sea.'

Tilly laughed. 'OK, good point. Now, why don't you tell me all about the progress you've made at the castello while I make us some dinner?'

Annie launched into a detailed breakdown of what she'd been doing in Tilly's absence and then her aunt filled her in on what she'd been up to on the other side of the island. It sounded as if Tilly would be away again soon and Annie would have to continue to make decisions on her own.

Rather than feeling daunted as she would have a few weeks ago, Annie felt a thrill of excitement. She'd found she loved being in charge.

Her phone began to ring. Leaving Tilly to finish making the dinner, she raced into the bedroom and eventually found her phone under the duvet.

'Molly!' she cried when she finally answered it.

'Hi, Mum. Why don't you keep your phone handier? I never think you're going to answer.'

'I hadn't realised I'd have a signal this evening. Is everything OK?'

Molly laughed. 'Yes, Mum. Apart from being robbed at gunpoint a few times this morning everything's fine. I'm off to the Students' Union.'

'Very funny. You wait until you have children.'

'I know ... I'll become a crazy woman too.' They both laughed. 'I was ringing to find out when you're coming home for Christmas.'

They chatted for a while before saying their goodbyes. Annie clutched the phone before dropping it back onto her bed. Their conversations always made her heart hurt a little. She missed her daughter so much — but she was so proud of her for getting into university. The two feelings warred within her sometimes.

Still, it wasn't long until they would both be home for Christmas, and they'd have nearly a month together. Annie couldn't wait.

9

'Are you pleased with how things are shaping up?' Ben asked Annie as they took their final stroll through the castle before they shut it up for the Christmas holidays.

Annie stopped in the hotel lobby. The light, airy space she'd envisaged was almost complete. Only the plug sockets needed to be screwed into place and then she could begin working on the decor. She'd ordered so many swatches and tester paint pots that she now had to clamber into bed to get past them. She couldn't bring them to the hotel to give her more space. The dust would ruin them within a day.

Her plan for the lobby was to leave the original stone untouched, with one wall plastered and decorated in understated colours as the backdrop for the reception desk. She'd found two large, elegant vases in a shop in Vescovina, a place from which she'd probably be buying quite a lot. She'd asked for them to be kept for her and she envisaged them standing on either side of the front entrance.

'I love it,' she said.

'Great,' said Ben as they both stepped outside. 'Well, I guess this is it for a few weeks. Have a lovely Christmas.'

He leaned forward and gave her an awkward hug and a kiss on the cheek. Annie squeezed him back — it was like hugging a tank, he was so solid. She'd miss his reassuring presence when his part of the project was over — which, if all went to schedule, would be late February or early March.

'See you next year,' called Annie cheerfully as Ben climbed into his van and disappeared down the track towards the town.

Her taxi to the airport wasn't due for a few hours so she left her bags inside the hotel and decided to head down to the Roman ruins. She loved the tranquillity of the ancient building, and went there often when she needed to think.

The wintry sun cast long shadows over the tumbledown walls of the Roman villa. Annie sat down in her favourite spot and mentally added her sketch pad to the list of things she was going to bring back with her from the UK. She'd love to capture the way the light turned the stones a soft golden colour. She bent down to get a better look at some of the stonework.

'What are you doing?' asked a low voice from behind her.

'Er, nothing,' she said, straightening up and turning to face Giovanni, whom she hadn't heard approach. 'I was just having a walk and I thought I saw an animal dash by here.'

'A lizard, possibly,' suggested Giovanni.

'Perhaps,' said Annie.

There was a long pause.

'I should …'

'Would you …?' they both began.

'No, go ahead,' said Annie as Giovanni gestured that she should speak. She'd been unsure of what to say, just wanted to end the silence before it became unbearably awkward.

'I was going to ask if you'd like some coffee.' Giovanni pulled a flask out of his rucksack.

Annie was so surprised, she found herself agreeing. Seconds later, as she leaned against a low wall with a small silver cup in her hand, she really wished she hadn't. She'd prolonged their awkward encounter by at least ten minutes. She had nothing to say to him — or he to her, by the looks of things. He leaned against the wall opposite her, tapping the mug with his fingers.

'So, did you read the stuff I gave you about the hotel development?' he asked eventually.

'Of course. I read it the day you gave it to me. And I thought you were on to something, but every avenue I've followed up is a dead end.'

'Where did you try?'

'The council, local builders and I even rang the hotel company you suspect of involvement. Everyone is denying all knowledge. It could be that my Italian isn't good enough to notice a fudge in the conversation. Perhaps you should try.'

'A fudge? Do you mean like a chocolate?'

Annie giggled. 'No. I mean a misdirection. You know, they could be putting me off by not telling me the whole truth and I'm not aware of it. I'm afraid I don't know where I can go with the investigation from here.'

Giovanni nodded and took a sip of his coffee. 'So,' he said finally, 'you are learning Italian. How is that going?'

'I know enough to say sorry to a man, should I ever head-butt one again.'

Giovanni grinned, changing his face so remarkably that Annie felt the breath whoosh out of her. Now she could see why girls got giggly when they saw him. Her heart skipped a few beats.

'Do you make a habit of attacking strangers with shopping baskets?' he asked.

'Not usually,' said Annie, smiling back at him. 'I —' She froze.

'What is it?' Giovanni glanced at her sharply.

'Something's happening up there.'

'Where?' said Giovanni, twisting round to see what she was looking at.

Annie stood and tugged him down with her behind the level of the nearest wall, spilling coffee over her fingers as she did so.

'Up the hill, on the scrubland between the castle and these ruins,' she whispered. 'There's a group of men. Some of them are in suits and others have those weird things on tripods.'

'What weird things?' Giovanni made to stand up but Annie pulled him back down.

'The instruments people use when they're assessing the height of land. At least that's what I've always assumed they're for.'

Giovanni stared at her. She could feel the heat of his arm through his long-sleeved T-shirt. She removed her hand.

'Are you thinking what I'm thinking?' she asked.

'I'm thinking we don't need to be hiding behind this wall.'

'We don't want them to see us.'

'Why not?'

'Because they have no good reason to be up there. They're nothing to do with the castle. They can only be there because of the hotel development. The one everyone is denying knowing anything about.'

'I still don't understand why we are hiding.' Annie shook her head in frustration.

'They've obviously waited until the castle's closed up for Christmas. They're hiding from us — so we should hide from them.'

Giovanni stayed crouching down but peered over the top of the wall.

'We should move closer,' he said. 'I may recognise some of them.'

He made to stand and she grabbed his arm again. He looked down at her.

'OK,' he said. 'We'll stay low, even though I'm not sure why we need to. We're not the ones with something to hide.'

He turned away from her and started a hunched walk. Annie couldn't help but giggle at his awkward posture. Giovanni turned and grinned at her.

'Would you like to go first?' he said, gesturing in front of him.

'No, it's OK. I'm happy to follow your lead.'

He narrowed his eyes into a glare but amusement still shone out of them so she was sure he wasn't really angry with her. She'd been the object of enough glowers from him to be able to tell the difference.

Progress was slow in their hunched positions but they eventually made it to part of the ruins closest to the area where the men were still gathered. It still wasn't close enough to hear what was being said but Annie could now make out detail on their faces.

'You're right,' said Giovanni. 'Those men are taking measurements of the landscape.'

Annie's stomach formed a hard knot.

'I really hoped I was wrong. Any development in that area, even a tiny hut, would detract from the beauty of the surrounding landscape.'

'I recognise some of the men,' said Giovanni softly. 'You see the bald man in the yellow suit?'

Annie leaned closer to Giovanni and got a waft of citrus aftershave.

'I see him,' she said quietly. She moved away from Giovanni; she shouldn't be noticing the way he smelled.

'He's the head of town planning at the council — Lorenzo Moretti.'

'No!' said Annie, moving forward to get another look. 'Oh no,' she said. 'It gets worse. It looks like they're telling my taxi driver to go away.'

As Annie watched in horror, the car she'd booked to take her to the airport turned around and headed away from the castle.

'Where were you going?' asked Giovanni.

'The airport.' She glanced at her watch. 'My flight home is in three hours.'

'My car's not far from here. Let's go.'

'What?' asked Annie, still staring up at

the castle in dismay. She'd been at the ruins far longer than she'd intended.

'I'll take you to the airport,' Giovanni clarified. 'You!

Why on earth would you do that?'

'Because I'm not completely horrible and it would be rude to leave you stranded when my car is a short walk away. Come on or we'll be late.'

Giovanni strode off, leaving Annie gaping at him. She could not get a handle on this mercurial man. After a few seconds she hurried after him, no longer caring if the men above them on the hill could see her. Getting to the airport so that she could see Molly tomorrow was far more important.

She caught up with him under the pine trees. He wasn't following any path but she trusted he wasn't luring her to a hidden hollow to murder her and leave her body. Obviously the thought had crossed her mind, otherwise she wouldn't be constantly reassuring herself that he was generally considered to be a good man and she'd been unlucky to see his grumpy side.

His car was old but clean, and she clambered in gratefully.

'Don't worry, I'll get you there on time,' he said as he turned the engine on and moved swiftly along narrow lanes.

'What will we do about the development?' she asked, to take her mind off the time.

He shrugged. 'A large hotel complex built there will destroy the local environment and rip apart one of the most tranquil parts of the island. But it could be good for some local businesses so we will probably find we're two of only a handful of people against the idea.'

'It seems the company behind the supposed development is called Global Hotel. If it is them, then it's not good news. They generally build huge hotels,' said Annie. 'When I was doing my research on them I didn't find one without at least three big pools. A hotel like that would ruin Tilly's idea of an idyllic retreat, too.'

Giovanni sped up the hill towards the

castle and pulled to a stop outside the main entrance. The men in suits were just climbing into their cars and ignored them totally as they stepped out of Giovanni's car.

Annie stopped to watch them leave. 'Quick,' said Giovanni when the last car had disappeared from sight. 'Let's grab your bags.'

'What should we do about Global Hotel?' asked Annie as she unlocked the door and stepped inside.

Annie hurried over to her suitcase and backpack as Giovanni stopped to take in the newly constructed foyer.

'Wow,' he said. 'You've done an amazing job here. The last time I came in here, it wasn't fit for rats to live in. Now it's beautiful.'

'Thank you,' said Annie, dragging her case across the floor.

'Let me,' said Giovanni trying to take the case from her.

After a brief tussle he managed to get the suitcase from her but she held on to the rucksack.

'Thank you for this,' she said as they got back in the car.

'No problem. In answer to your question earlier, I don't know what we can do about the hotel.'

'We could call a town meeting.'

He smiled across at her. 'We could.'

'Will you wait until I get back? I'd like to be there.'

'Yes, I will. No one will be interested in doing anything now, anyway. Not when it is time for Christmas and New Year celebrations.'

'I'll contact you when I get back, then,' she said, settling back and trying to relax. She kept her eyes fixed on the horizon as if this would help them arrive quicker. The knot in her stomach hadn't eased. If they didn't stop the hotel development, then all her efforts to turn the castello into a beautiful rural retreat would be wasted and her first foray into paid work would end in disaster.

10

'Annie, I'm over here!' Looking over, she saw Tilly waving madly to attract her attention.

It wasn't really necessary as there were only a handful of other people waiting for passengers in the almost empty airport and with her colourful beads and ribbons she was by far the most distinctive person in the room.

Annie was so pleased to see her aunt that as she reached her, she flung her arms around her. Christmas had been in parts, blissful and in others, sad. She and Molly had decided to stop renting the little terraced house they'd called home for several years. It made no sense to pay rent on it when neither of them was living there.

They'd packed up their belongings and left them in storage.

Annie had bought a large box and placed in it all of Molly's school reports and artwork she'd done over the years. Molly had laughed at her, but Annie wasn't ready to let them go. The tears she'd shed on the way to Italy had been bittersweet, but she was ready for the challenge of the hotel now and looking forward to getting on with the next stage.

'Oh, love, how are you?' asked Tilly, rubbing Annie's back through her thick padded coat.

'I'm fine. I'm already missing Molly but she was so excited to be heading back to university that I'm glad to be back here and to have something to take my mind of not being with her all the time.'

Annie released Tilly and stood back a little to look at her.

'Do you want to go straight to the cottage or do you want to get a coffee?' Tilly reached up and pushed some of Annie's hair away from her face.

'Let's go straight to the cottage. I'd like to stretch my legs and visit the castle. I've missed it so much.'

There was no queue for the taxi and

so they were soon zooming along the motorway towards their temporary home.

The cottage was just how she'd left it. She sat on the edge of the bed and looked at the pictures of Molly she'd stuck to the wall. She lightly touched a picture of Molly beaming with pleasure over the size of an ice cream and smiled.

New covers were on the bed, and the tiny bedside table was dust-free. Tilly had obviously prepared for her arrival and Annie was grateful. She didn't have the energy to tidy right now.

She curled up on the bed and sank into the mattress, the muscles in her neck and shoulders relaxing as she did so ...

'Are you ready?' called Tilly. Annie leapt off the bed.

'In a sec,' she called back.

She pulled a clean pair of jeans and a thick jumper out of her case and changed quickly. She'd unpack properly later.

'Have you been practising your Italian?' asked Tilly as they walked towards the town.

'I have. I want to organise a town meeting about this proposed development and so I've been trying to learn vocabulary around that. It's difficult to know what's going to come up, though. I'm hoping Carlotta and Greta will come along with me and help if I get stuck.'

'Are you sure about this hotel development, then? Has something else happened to convince you that I don't know about?' Tilly asked, a small crease forming between her eyebrows.

'I don't know about anything since I've been away but I'd say what Giovanni and I witnessed was pretty strong evidence that something surreptitious is going on there.'

Annie described what she'd seen but Tilly still didn't seem to be convinced.

'I still think we should find out more before you instigate a town meeting,' said Tilly.

'What else do you think I need to find out?' asked Annie, confused as to why Tilly didn't seem to be taking the threat as seriously as it warranted. As far as she was concerned, there was enough evidence to suggest that something secretive was going on. In her experience secrets did not lead to good things.

'Don't be grumpy with me, darling. I'm just saying that we need concrete evidence before we call a town meeting. We don't want to cause unpleasant feeling and unrest for no reason.'

Annie considered her aunt's comments. She'd been so sure that something bad was happening that she hadn't stopped to think what would happen if she was wrong.

'You're right, of course,' she said as they arrived at Carlotta's apartment. 'I'll talk to Giovanni and see whether he has any further evidence. It may be something we can tackle on our own without involving anyone else.'

11

The lobby was finished and ready for decorating. It was a thrill for Annie to finally dip her paint roller into fresh paint and get stuck into covering the walls in her chosen colours.

Her days became endless coatings of primer and paint and, despite her assurances that she'd contact Giovanni, the weeks sped by and she'd pushed all thought of the hotel development to one side.

She barely had any energy, anyway. At the end of every day she managed to stagger into the shower to scrub off the layer of paint that had settled on her and then to collapse into bed where she would sleep deeply until the morning when she would start the whole cycle again.

Then finally, in early February, the painting of the ground floor of the castle was finished.

Standing with Tilly in the centre of the lobby, Annie felt a lump form in her throat.

'It's beautiful,' said Tilly softly.

'I know,' Annie said, half-laughing, half-crying.

'You're a genius with colours.'

'I know,' said Annie again, this time laughing out loud.

They spun slowly around, looking at the crisply painted panelling and the exposed brickwork.

'I love those vases,' said Tilly, pointing to the tall, narrow pots Annie had placed either side of the entrance.

'I think they should be filled with local flowers,' said Annie. 'During the winter months you could use fake ones, but during the summer they should be real. I rang a farmer who lives about twenty kilometres away from here and he is going to email us a quote for supplying flowers on a weekly basis. He's supplying other hotels on the island and so I went to see his arrangements. I think, if he's not too extortionate, he'll be worth contracting.'

'Thank you, Annie. You've done an excellent job so far. I'm looking forward to seeing the rest of the rooms as they're finished. Also, I've been meaning to talk to you about... oh, hello, can I help you?'

Annie turned to see whom Tilly was addressing. 'Ciao,' she said when she realised who had come through the front entrance of the hotel.

'Tilly, this is Carlotta's brother, Giovanni.'

Although Tilly had been emailing Giovanni about selling some of the castle's land to him, they had never met. Annie felt a fluttering in her stomach as they regarded each other solemnly. For some reason it was important to her that they got on well, and it wasn't just because of the land sale.

Giovanni and Tilly shook hands politely.

Giovanni cleared his throat. He seemed uncomfortable under Tilly's intense gaze.

'You've done a great job in here,' he commented, looking around the room.

'Thank you,' said Annie, waiting to see what he was going to say next.

They hadn't seen each other since he'd dropped her off at the airport nearly two months ago. She'd hoped this was due to the fact that he had nothing to report on the development. His arrival at the hotel did not bode well.

Or had he come to ask them to move out of the cottage? He'd be within his rights to do so if he'd found someone who would pay to live in the space. Either way her stomach knotted.

'I thought I should let you both know,' he said, 'that a friend of mine, who owns a hotel in the next town along, has some guests staying who will be of interest to you both.'

'Oh?' said Tilly.

'One of them is the head of Global Hotel's regional development projects. This isn't a guess as this is what he filled in on his hotel registration form. It also isn't a family holiday. The other guests staying with him are clearly businessmen. My contact told me they were talking over dinner last night about their latest project on the island and Vescovina was mentioned several times.'

Tilly leaned against the newly polished reception desk. Annie felt her heart start to beat uncomfortably fast.

No one said anything for a moment.

'Annie, do you still have the print-out — you know the one, which shows the size of Global Hotel's newest proposed development?' Tilly asked.

'Yes,' said Annie numbly. 'I'll go and get it from the office.'

The office was still a shell of a room but it had electricity, so Annie had started to do all her paperwork in there.

All her research, which wasn't much, on the suspected development was stacked neatly on top of a couple of tins of paint. She took the whole file back into the lobby. Flipping the file open she riffled through the paper before pulling out an A4 sheet.

'This is it,' she said.

The three of them leaned over the piece of paper and Annie caught a whiff

120

of Giovanni's unique citrus scent. She stepped back. She wished she'd stop noticing how good he smelled.

'Here,' she said, thrusting the paper at Tilly. 'I've looked at it enough times to know it will be a disaster for us. You can take a closer look.'

Tilly looked up at her and frowned but fortunately didn't comment on her slightly sharp comment. She wished Tilly had taken the threat more seriously earlier. Perhaps they could have nipped the whole thing in the bud before Global Hotel had sent a representative out here.

'Why don't we go outside and take a look at the area?' Tilly suggested. 'It might not be as bad as we are all thinking.'

They traipsed outside.

Tilly held the printed sheet out in front of her so they could all see it.

'I don't think,' said Annie after a moment's study, 'that there is any way this development is going to be good for the castello. Even though we're on a slope, those tower blocks —' she tapped the paper — 'the ones which will clearly make up the hotel bedrooms — are still going to block out our views of the sea and the ruins. They'll be all we'll be able to see from here, even from the highest point in the castle. My roof-top pool won't be as romantic as I'd planned.'

Annie touched the paper where two large apartment blocks were outlined. They were each six storeys tall with balconies for each room. On one side, the balconies would look straight out on to the castello.

Tilly nodded slowly.

'It would also destroy all this lovely natural habitat,' said Tilly, her voice hoarse as she waved her hands to encompass everything they could see before them.

Finally Tilly was beginning to see the enormity of the problem.

'It will be a disaster for the wildlife, which in turn will have a negative impact on my farm,' said Giovanni flatly. 'And it will be an eye-pain.'

'I think you mean eyesore,' said Annie,

smiling in spite of the situation.

Giovanni's lips twitched but he didn't turn to her. 'That as well,' he said gravely.

'What do we do?' asked Tilly.

'I think it's time for that town meeting,' said Annie decisively. 'Do you think we could gather enough support against the hotel, Giovanni?'

'I don't think the hotel will be popular amongst my generation and older. I'm not sure about the younger people. They might feel that the benefits outweigh the negatives.'

'What on earth are the benefits?' asked Tilly incredulously.

'A new, large hotel will bring in lots of local jobs,' said Annie.

'There's that,' said Giovanni, 'but there is also the possibility of an improved nightlife. Vescovina is not particularly exciting if you're young. A steady influx of young men and women would also be appealing to some.'

They fell silent again.

Somewhere from inside the castello Tilly's phone began to ring.

'I'd best go and see who that is,' said Tilly. 'It could be the estate agent finally getting back to me.' She disappeared inside.

'Is your aunt planning to put the castello back on the market?' Giovanni asked, his shoulders rigid and his eyes fixed on a distant point.

'No, of course not. She loves this hotel. I think it's her favourite project so far. Why do you ask?'

'The estate agent calling,' Giovanni stated.

'Oh, that. She's put an offer on an old hotel on the other side of the island. It's nothing like this one, just a run of the mill hotel that's gone a bit ropey. The vendors are holding off waiting for her to offer more. I don't think they'll get a better offer from anyone else and Tilly's not going to increase the amount she's willing to pay. I know she looks flaky but she's actually a very astute businesswoman. I think that takes people by surprise.'

Giovanni let out a long breath and he

turned to look at her.

'What happens if they do accept? Will she give this up?' He gestured to the castle behind them.

'No, I've already told you she loves it. Why do you keep thinking we're going to give up?'

Giovanni pushed his hand through his hair and looked out towards the sea again.

'You're the only person who's taken me seriously about this hotel development. I don't want to lose you.'

To Annie's surprise Giovanni's ears turned pink but he kept his gaze firmly on the distant Mediterranean.

'Why is it so important to you?' asked Annie.

Giovanni's ears turned redder and he ran his hands through his hair again.

'I don't want hordes of people running around and potentially contaminating my farm,' he said eventually.

He seemed poised to say more so she waited for him to elaborate but he didn't continue.

'OK,' she said eventually. 'I think we're both agreed that a town meeting is the best way forward. Can you ask people you think might be against the idea if they would be willing to come along to one?'

'Yes,' he said, his sea-blue gaze returning to her. 'I'm sure that Carlotta would be happy to open up her shop so we could hold it there.'

'Don't you think it will be a bit crowded?'

Annie couldn't imagine having a good conversation around the stacks of aubergines and lumpy peppers.

'She sometimes has special food evenings. Everything is pushed to one side and then people come and taste new products. There's a lot of good food and some aperitivi. They're popular with local people. I'm sure if we offered something similar, we'd have a good turnout.'

'Wouldn't people then be turning up for the food and the drink?'

'That would be part of the draw, yes. But I think we'll get a better response than if we ask people just to come and talk about the development. Like your aunt Tilly, I don't think anyone will take it seriously until they see the first bricks being laid down. By then, it will be too late.'

'OK,' said Annie. 'It sounds like a good idea.'

'I'll speak to Carlotta and organise a date. I'd better have your number so we can arrange what we want to get out of the meeting.'

'Sure,' said Annie.

He pulled his phone out of his pocket and she gave him her details. A strange, fluttery sensation started up around her heart but she quashed it. This was all about business — he wasn't asking for her number so he could take her out on a date. She must remember that. A man who looked like him would not be interested in a woman who looked like her.

12

Annie dipped her paintbrush in the pot of thick, glossy paint. She'd started decorating with such enthusiasm but she'd quickly got bored with all the skirting boards that needed such care.

When she'd got back to the cottage later that night, she was going to take another look at the budget she'd drawn up. Surely she could squeeze out some more money to pay for someone to come and do this for her?

Her phone rang and she fumbled with the paintbrush as she tried to reach it.

'Hello,' she said just before it rang off.

'Buongiorno, Annie. It's Giovanni.'

'Oh, hello, I mean ... buongiorno.'

She heard Giovanni's soft laugh. What was it about this man that made her lose her ability with language? Greta said she was the fastest student she'd ever taught but Giovanni made her revert back to basics.

'I have spoken with Carlotta about having a town meeting in her shop and she is happy with the idea,' he said.

Annie already knew this, having had dinner with Carlotta yesterday evening, but Carlotta said they'd not decided on a date yet. She said as much to Giovanni.

'We've agreed to have it on Friday,' he told her.

'In four days' time!' Annie exclaimed. 'Is that really enough time for us to get organised?'

'I know it doesn't give us much time,' he agreed. 'But I think we need to move quickly if we're to have a hope of preventing this disaster.'

She couldn't argue with that.

'Are you free tonight? Carlotta and I are going to plan what to say and I think you and Tilly should be involved.'

'Tilly's on the other side of the island for a few days dealing with her other hotel but I'm available. What time shall I meet you at Carlotta's?'

'It will have to be at my house, I'm afraid. I've no one to look after Serena

129

and I don't want to take her out after her bedtime. I'll provide food, or Carlotta will. She's better at cooking than I am.'

'Of course,' said Annie, who was desperate to see Giovanni's house. 'What's your address?'

'Just turn right out of your cottage and follow the bend in the road. Keep going and you'll come to it in about ten minutes.'

Annie hadn't realised they lived so close. She always turned the other way out of her cottage to walk into the town, or headed straight up the hill in front of her to get to the castello.

'OK, I'll see you later,' she said.

'Ciao,' said Giovanni and then he was gone.

★ ★ ★

It was dark by the time Annie arrived at the two-storey farmhouse. Giovanni must be doing well with his farm, because the building was the largest Annie had seen around the small town. Or perhaps it was the modelling that had paid him generously. Either way it was a beautiful-looking home with arched windows typical of the area running down its length.

A small wind stirred the branches of a wispy tree that framed the entrance as she knocked on the front door.

'Hey,' said Giovanni as he pulled open the door. 'Please come in.'

She'd never seen him so dishevelled. His white shirt was untucked from pale blue jeans. His feet were bare and Annie found herself mesmerised by them as she followed him into the house.

She stood for a moment at the kitchen door. This was the kitchen she'd always dreamed of owning herself. Unlike the galley one she was used to in Britain, this was wide and long with a large wooden table at its centre.

A pot bubbling over on the hob caught her attention as water hit the gas and let off an angry hiss of steam.

Giovanni let off a stream of swear words in Italian as he rushed over to turn down the heat. 'Sorry,' he said, his neck flushing red. 'I forgot you understand Italian now.' Annie laughed.

'I wouldn't call myself fluent but I understood enough of what you said to realise you're not very happy with that pot.'

Giovanni grinned and Annie's stomach flipped in response.

'I was hoping to be calmly laying the table when you arrived but Serena had a nightmare and I had to go and comfort her.'

'She's more important than a few knives and forks. I can lay the table if you point me in the direction of the cutlery.'

'Thanks. It's in that drawer over there,' said Giovanni, waving a wooden spoon in the direction of the other end of the kitchen. 'And it's only the two of us. Carlotta rang to tell me that she's got to take Sofia to her rehearsals. Her husband is stuck at work. She's going to try and come over later but she's going to miss dinner.'

Annie opened the drawer Giovanni had pointed to and pulled it open. She stared at the cutlery for a moment as her mind reeled at the thought of spending a cosy evening with Giovanni in his stunning kitchen.

She shook her head. This wasn't a romantic interlude. They were together to plan their fight for the land, and she wasn't sure he even liked her that much. As he'd told her, she was the only person he'd met who was as against Global Hotel as he was — which made them allies but not necessarily friends.

She pulled out two sets of forks and knives. 'Will we need spoons?' she asked.

'Yeah, it's carbonara. And it's nearly ready.'

At the table she dithered over where they should sit. Next to one another seemed to suggest romance, but the table was so large that sitting opposite one another would be ridiculous. They'd have to shout to make themselves heard. In the end she settled for placing him at the head and her to his right. She allowed enough space so that there was no chance of accidentally bumping arms or legs.

She sat in her place just as he was placing plates piled high with spaghetti coated in a silky carbonara sauce.

'This smells amazing,' she said, touching it lightly with her fork.

'I hope it's edible,' he said. 'I'm not as good a cook as Carlotta.'

She twirled a mouthful onto her fork and took a large bite. It was just the right blend of salty bacon and garlic.

'It's perfect,' she said.

'Papà,' said a tiny voice from the doorway.

'Serena, what are you doing down here again?' Giovanni asked in Italian.

'I had a bad dream,' Serena mumbled sleepily. 'You've not had time to sleep, my lovely girl. You can't have had another dream yet.'

Serena padded over to the table and lifted her arms up, waiting for her father to pull her onto his lap. He sighed gently, but did as she requested. She snuggled against his chest, pulled a section of his shirt into her fist and stuck her thumb into her mouth.

'Sorry,' he mouthed over his daughter's head.

Annie smiled at him and carried on eating her dinner. She tried to remind herself of how grumpy he'd been to her for months and how many times he'd glowered at her during that time. She did not want to think about how gorgeous he looked with his small daughter curled against his solid chest. Over the soft clink of cutlery on plates, Serena's eyelids slowly began to drop closed.

'Is she asleep?' Giovanni whispered.

Annie looked at the little girl, whose thumb was now only hanging loosely in her mouth.

'I think so,' she said softly.

'If I carry her, could you open doors for me?'

'Of course,' she said, pushing her chair away from the table as quietly as she could manage.

She hoped her pleasure at being able to see more of the house wasn't evident on her face.

Outside the kitchen Giovanni headed down a long corridor, then up some wooden stairs. Annie slipped off her shoes and followed him.

He stopped at the top and said, 'Her room's the third on the right. If you could pull down the covers on her bed, that'd be great.'

Serena's room was decorated in pale pinks and purples. Soft toys were scattered across the mattress and the pillow. Annie moved a few out of the way and Giovanni settled Serena on the bed. Not wanting to intrude on the private moment, Annie left him to it. She heard a soft murmur of 'Papà' as she padded back down the corridor. She glanced into the next room but scurried on when she realised it must be Giovanni's bedroom. She didn't want to be caught snooping. She did notice that only one side of the bed was unmade and wondered, not for the first time, where Ashley, Giovanni's glamorous wife, was. She'd not met her in the six months she'd been living in Italy and Carlotta never talked about her. Neither did Giovanni, for that matter.

She made her way back to the kitchen and wandered over to the fridge. There was a picture of Giovanni and Serena at the beach and lots of brightly coloured paintings covering it, but nothing to show that Ashley lived here too.

Feeling guilty about snooping, she washed the dishes and placed them on the draining board. When she had finished scrubbing the pans there was still no sign of Giovanni. After five more minutes she decided to go back to her cottage.

She went into the hallway to locate her trainers and met Giovanni creeping down the stairs.

'I'm so sorry,' he said quietly. 'She woke and wanted me to stay with her.'

'Don't worry. I remember that time well. Although it seems endless and exhausting, try to enjoy it while she still wants to spend lots of time with you. It stops soon enough.'

'Is your daughter older, then?' asked

Giovanni as they walked back into the kitchen.

Annie laughed, 'Oh goodness, yes. I wouldn't be in Italy if Molly was still a child. I didn't even like to leave her to do the weekly shop until she was in her mid-teens. Molly's eighteen and started university in September.'

Giovanni's double take was comical.

'How old are you?' he asked in confusion. Annie laughed again and a blush swept across his high cheekbones.

'I'm sorry. I'm not supposed to ask that, am I? I thought you were younger than me. You certainly look it,' he explained, staring at her as if the answer was written across her forehead.

'I'm thirty-eight,' she said. 'Oh, right,' said Giovanni.

'I had Molly about a week after my twentieth birthday. My husband and I were childhood sweethearts. Some people disapproved of us getting married and starting a family so young, but I'm very glad we did. He died when Molly was five and although that's a tragedy, we did get five very happy years as a family of three.'

'Right,' said Giovanni again.

Annie couldn't read his expression. He seemed to be fighting an internal battle. Then he noticed the state of the kitchen through the open doorway. 'You cleared up.' He groaned. 'You didn't need to do that.'

'It was the least I could do after you cooked.'

'This evening has been a disaster. All you've had is a mediocre meal, which you had to eat in silence, and then you've had to clean it all up by yourself.' He ran his fingers through his hair. 'Let's go through to the salone and have a brandy. I lit a fire before you arrived and so the room should be warm by now. We can talk in comfort in there.'

* * *

The embers of the fire were glowing red as they made their way into the living room. Giovanni threw a couple of logs in it and used a poker to get the flames going again. Annie sat in a squishy arm chair in front of it and warmed her toes.

Giovanni handed her a drink and she accepted it gratefully.

'Will Serena sleep through now?' asked Annie. 'I hope so,' said Giovanni, taking a sip of his drink. 'She never used to wake up like this. Ashley and I were very smug because she slept through the night when she was only twelve weeks old.'

'What changed?'

Giovanni watched the flames for a long moment and Annie thought he wasn't going to answer.

'Ashley left,' he said eventually. 'Almost a year ago she had a call from our old agent. A producer had seen her face and they wanted her to audition for an American soap opera. To cut a long story short, she went and got the part.

'I'd spent five hard years getting the farm how I wanted it and we were finally beginning to turn a profit. I didn't want to jack it in and move back to America.'

He laughed sadly.

'It turns out she didn't want me to go with her. That I can kind of understand — but she didn't want Serena to go either. It was Ashley's childhood dream to become a Hollywood actress. Being a wife and mother stuck in rural Italy didn't fit into the fantasy.

'The only saving grace is that she's American and we got married in Los Angeles which means she was able to divorce me quickly. She's granted me full custody of Serena so I don't need to worry about that.

'I'm grateful for that because I don't have to share my daughter and send her off to America for half the year, but...'

The bleakness in Giovanni's eyes as he watched the flickering fire made Annie want to reach across and take hold of his hands.

'I'm so angry, Annie.'

His gaze suddenly met hers and she was shocked by the raw pain she saw in his expression. 'Not for me. If she wants to leave me, good luck to her. But how can she leave her daughter? I don't understand and I'll never forgive her for the pain she's causing Serena.'

He looked at the fire. Annie was lost for words. Giovanni gave a snort of laughter.

'And once again I'm sorry. I bet you were thinking this evening couldn't get any worse and then I unburden my messy life.'

Annie didn't laugh in response.

'I wouldn't be able to forgive her either,' said Annie quietly.

Giovanni paused and then nodded, 'Thank you,' he said.

The fire crackled gently in front of them.

Let's discuss Global Hotel and Friday's meeting,' said Giovanni briskly, sitting upright in his chair. It seemed the time for confidences was over. 'I think part of the problem we have is that they've yet to submit formal plans, so we're currently fighting a ghost. We need to list all the reasons we're convinced it's happening and why we think it's such a

142

bad idea for the community.'

He leaned over the side of his arm-chair and picked up a pad of paper.

The fire was dying and Annie's head was reeling. It wasn't just the effects of the brandy. Giovanni had tried to teach her some of the more technical Italian but it hadn't stuck in her mind like it did when Greta taught her. It could be that Greta was the better teacher but Annie had a horrible feeling it might be because her brain was full up of images of Giovanni's face as it was lit up by the flickering firelight.

'I think I'm done for this evening,' she said, after she'd resisted the temptation to sweep his hair back from his face for the tenth time.

'Right,' said Giovanni, looking up from his paper and glancing at his watch. 'I hadn't realised how late it's become. Do you need to be up early tomorrow?'

'I've got to be up early every morning. I've got so much to get done before the first guests arrive.'

'Have you already got bookings?' asked

Giovanni as she stood up and stretched.

'Tilly had our first booking this week for a yoga retreat in early June, for every room in the hotel. I need to get cracking if I'm to finish in time.'

They wandered back into the hallway and Annie slipped on her shoes. Giovanni held out her coat and she slid her arms in. His fingers brushed the nape of her neck and she shuddered at the unintentional contact.

'If there's anything I can do to help ...'

'Thanks. If you can hurry up and buy the land from Tilly, I can use some of the cash to pay towards a painter and decorator. That way I won't have to paint the whole castle myself.'

'You're painting every room!'

'Yeah, there's nothing in the budget to pay for another person. Believe me, I've been over the figures so many times desperate to find a few euro to pay for someone else.'

'I can't hurry up my solicitor any more than I have tried to do already, but I could certainly come over and help you do some decorating. My parents are having Serena for a sleepover on Friday night and taking her to see their friends the day after, so I could come and help you on Saturday.'

'You don't have to give up your free time for that,' said Annie, who didn't think spending more time with Giovanni was a good idea. 'I can't pay you,' she added.

He grinned, a slow sexy grin and Annie's heart stuttered. 'I don't need the money but I do need someone to help me fight Global Hotel. Take this as my way of keeping you onside.'

'OK, thanks. I'll be off now,' said Annie, wrenching open the front door and stepping into the cool night air. She took a deep breath hoping it would knock some sense into her.

His lopsided grin was making her insides squirm. If she didn't get away from him, there was no telling what crazy things she would do.

'Do you have a car?' Giovanni asked as she made to walk off.

'No, that's not in my budget either.' She pulled her jacket sleeves over her fingers.

'I could lend you my old moped,' he offered.

Annie wished Giovanni would stop being so kind. If she could go back to thinking he was arrogant and rude, it would make life a lot easier. 'Thanks but I don't think I could accept that,' she said. 'I always told Molly she wasn't allowed a motorbike and I think it's best to practise what you preach.'

Giovanni laughed. 'It's only a 50cc. I doubt you'd be able to go much over thirty miles an hour on it. It would certainly make your life easier. Go on... live a little.'

'Thanks, I'll think about it,' said Annie, who was planning to do no such thing. All motorbikes were death traps in her eyes, including mopeds. She marched back to the cottage, running when she was no longer in sight of the farmhouse.

How embarrassing to be having lustful thoughts about Carlotta's brother.

She was such a cliché — a middle-aged widow who was crushing on the town's most handsome resident. She'd been so young when she'd met Hugo that she could barely remember what it was like to be attracted to another man. Perhaps that's all these strange and unwanted feelings were; her hormones were going wild after years of being repressed.

She'd have to make sure he never knew. She couldn't live with the embarrassment of being found out to be like every other female on the island.

13

'Stop fidgeting,' whispered Carlotta. 'You are making me nervous.'

'I can't help it. I wasn't expecting so many people to turn up.'

'Everyone wants to eat my food,' said Carlotta. 'You shouldn't be surprised.'

'This isn't about your food,' said Annie, shuffling from foot to foot as she watched the crowd forming in Carlotta's shop.

Along one wall Carlotta had set up several trestle tables, which were groaning under the weight of food she'd prepared. They'd sold the evening to locals as an opportunity to sample some of Carlotta's new food range while attending a town meeting. Annie was surprised at the size of the turnout. She'd been expecting about ten people but it was probably closer to a hundred packed into the shop.

'Some people will only be here for the food,' confirmed Greta, who was standing on the other side of Annie. 'At least half the women will be here to see Giovanni. That probably leaves us with about quarter of the people in the room who are genuinely interested in what you have to say about Global Hotel.'

Carlotta rolled her eyes and Annie felt heat creep up the back of her neck. She used her pad of paper to cool the air in front of her face. It wouldn't do to start blushing whenever Giovanni's name was mentioned. Greta would be remorseless in teasing Annie if she suspected her of even the tiniest of lustful thoughts.

'Surely some of them are here because of Global Hotel?' she asked, her voice coming out way too high-pitched.

'Stop worrying,' said Carlotta, patting her arm reassuringly. 'It will go well.'

She bustled off to the tables to help Sofia and her friends, who were employed for the evening to hand out the food, but who were becoming a little overwhelmed by the amount of people demanding their plates be filled at the same time.

'Have some wine,' said Greta, thrusting a glass into Annie's hands. 'It will calm your nerves.'

Annie took a large gulp from the glass and immediately started spluttering.

'You're supposed to sip it slowly,' said Greta disapprovingly. 'You British have no appreciation of fine wine.'

Annie could only frown at her friend over her coughs.

'Is everything all right, Annie?' asked Giovanni, coming over to their side of the room.

Great — the first time he'd seen her this evening and she looked like a choking beetroot. Not that she cared how she looked, of course.

'Fine,' she managed to croak. 'A little nervous but fine.'

'She cannot handle her wine,' smirked Greta, flicking her curly hair over one shoulder. It seemed to be her reflex action every time Giovanni was in the vicinity.

Annie managed to pull in a huge lungful of air. 'I'm fine,' she said again, this time her voice actually sounding normal.

'Are you all set?' she asked Giovanni.

On Monday night they'd agreed that he would start things off and explain what they suspected. They would then try and gauge how many people were on the same side as them. If there was enough support they would outline what they had planned and ask for any other ideas.

'Yeah, I'm ready. I'll give everyone enough time to eat some of Carlotta's food and then I'll get on with it.'

'How's Serena?' she asked.

'Excited to be spending the weekend with my parents,' he said with a smile.

'Do you know what's happened to Ashley?' whispered Greta as Giovanni was pulled away by a group of smiling women.

'I don't,' lied Annie.

'She hasn't been seen for some time,' said Greta. 'I wonder if something's wrong — and I'm not the only one. See all those women circling — they're lining up to step into Ashley's shoes.'

'They look like vultures,' remarked

Annie. Greta snorted with laughter.

'Exactly like vultures,' she agreed.
'Shall we help Carlotta?' asked Annie.

She wanted to change the subject. She didn't like lying to her new friend but she guessed Giovanni didn't want people knowing about Ashley.

His divorce would have to come out sooner or later because they were bound to get the American soap opera over here. Alternatively, the islanders might start to think that Giovanni had murdered his wife and hidden her body underneath his olive trees. Either way, she didn't want to be the one who spilled the beans and ruined her tenuous friendship with Giovanni.

Her stomach was so tight with nerves that she didn't think she'd be able to eat anything. Then she saw Carlotta's spread.

She'd been expecting something akin to children's party food but this was far more sophisticated. Carlotta had cooked a huge range of different dishes served in giant pots. Guests were taking a plate

from one end of the table and working their way down, with Sofia and her
friends helping them to a little of every
dish as they went.

Behind each dish Carlotta was displaying the ingredients, which could be
bought at her shop. Annie picked up a
skewer of tiny meatballs and noticed a
stack of little cards beside the serving
pot. She picked one up and realised it
was the recipe for the meal she was eating. What a clever idea. She moved down
the table, trying all the dishes and col-
lecting all the recipe cards.

'Hey,' said a deep voice from behind
her. Annie turned to see Giovanni smiling at her.

He leaned down and said in a low
voice, 'I think some people are only here
for the food.'

He raised his eyebrows and glanced
down at her full plate. She laughed.

'For a moment I totally forgot why we
were here. I knew Carlotta was a good
cook from the amount of meals she's
made me but I didn't realise she was this

good. Why isn't she working as a professional cook?'

Annie picked up the skewer of meatballs and tried one from the top. She moaned softly.

'This tastes amazing. What is in it? It can't just be beef.'

Giovanni's gaze flicked to her mouth and quickly away again. He cleared his throat.

'I think she adds ham and some herbs. I'm not sure. Carlotta's good at cooking because she did train as a chef, but she didn't enjoy working the long hours. When Sofia came along she gave it up and opened her shop. This way she gets to spend time with Sofia and indulge in cooking for the masses every now and again.'

Annie had difficulty swallowing. Had she imagined him looking at her mouth? She didn't think so, but what could it possibly mean? There was no way a man who looked like Giovanni could find someone like her attractive.

'Are you OK?' he asked.

'Yes,' she squeaked. 'I mean, yes. I'm all good. I'm a bit nervous. I hadn't expected so many people to turn up.'

'I'll do all the talking,' he said. 'You just make a note of everyone who's interested in helping.'

'Great! I'll go and get a pen and paper.'

She hurried away from him. She wanted this sudden inconvenient attraction to stop. Aside for making her act like a teenager, it was ridiculous. He was a model and, although she knew she wasn't hideous, she certainly couldn't compete with all the female models he must have met. Not to mention the gorgeous women here tonight who all had their eyes on him. She didn't stand a chance — and she couldn't go forming a relationship with someone who lived in Italy.

Carlotta tapped a wine glass and the room gradually fell silent. Giovanni tipped over a crate and stood on it so that he could be seen by everyone. Annie noticed that the women who had been crowding round him earlier had somehow managed to be in front of him now.

'Look at those women,' hissed Carlotta as she appeared by Annie's side. 'It was like that growing up. Some of them are even the same people. If he didn't want them then, he's not going to want them now, is he? They are ridiculous.'

'Mmm,' Annie agreed.

Carlotta could never know that Annie found her brother attractive. She didn't want her best friend on the island to find her ridiculous.

Giovanni began talking and although it was in Italian, Annie followed most of what was being said. He explained the situation succinctly and explained that he and Annie were against the possible build. At this, a few people turned to look in her direction and Annie forced a smile that she hoped looked friendly but suspected made her look constipated. Giovanni ended by saying that he hoped he had everyone's support and asking for those against the development to leave their details.

A few people got up and left.

'Builders,' said Carlotta in her ear. 'Probably hoping to get some work out of the development. They can't be seen to be opposing Global Hotel, not if their livelihood depends on it. I don't know why they came in the first place. Perhaps they wanted to find out if we have concrete proof that the build is going ahead.'

'Let's hope all they wanted was some of your lovely food,' whispered Annie. 'And not that they were spying on us as the opposition.'

A fierce debate now seemed to be raging and Annie lost the thread of the conversation.

'What are they saying?' she asked Carlotta. 'They're discussing whether or not there's enough evidence to suggest a build is going to be proposed and if so what are the pros and cons of such a development. It's nothing we've not already thought of. By the sounds of things we're going to have about ten supporters, plus those women, who'll probably join up to get close to my brother. The idiots.'

'Only ten?' Annie looked around the

packed room.

'More people are against the idea than I thought would be. Some don't believe it's going to happen. Others don't believe we can fight the council or they don't want to try because they believe it's a waste of time.'

'But if we can prove it will have a negative impact on the environment then surely the council will have to be stopped,' Annie protested.

'That may be how it works where you come from but here, whoever has the biggest wallet wins.'

'Then this is hopeless.'

'Not hopeless but very difficult and, in the end, probably futile.'

Annie leaned against the wall. All those early mornings and late nights painting the castello's walls suddenly caught up with her. Her legs felt leaden and she wanted to crawl into bed. More than anything, she wanted to be away from all these people.

More people left as the debate drew to a close. Annie felt tears prick the back of her eyes as they went without giving her their details. The evening had been a complete waste of effort and she felt drained her of all her remaining energy.

In the end, only eight people left pledging their support, although Giovanni had also taken down the names and telephone numbers of the women who had been hanging around him all evening. Annie didn't believe they could rely on them for their help and she said as much to Carlotta. Carlotta snorted as she quickly tidied away the remains of the buffet.

'I doubt it too,' she said. 'No, there's no need for you to help, so please put that down. You look dead on your feet. Giovanni,' she called. 'You said you were going to take Annie home. Can you do it now, please? I think she's about to fall asleep on the vegetables.'

'You'll have to stay awake a bit longer,' said Giovanni. 'I've got the moped. I thought I could drive you back on it and leave it at yours for you to ride.'

Annie snapped upright. 'I really

don't think —'

'I'll drive like a snail,' he said, grinning at her. Annie badly wanted to go home but she was terrified of getting on a motorbike — and of getting closer to Giovanni than was wise.

'I don't have a helmet,' she protested weakly.

'I have a spare,' he answered. 'You're not getting away with it that easily. Come on.'

He propelled her out of the shop and handed her a black helmet twice the size of her head.

'There's no visor,' she said, feeling around the top in the hope that one would appear.

He laughed again.

'It's a moped,' he said. 'You don't need a visor. Come on, you big coward. Get on.'

'But aren't you going to drive?' she said, as he didn't move to get on first.

'Yeah, I'll drive — but you need to get on and then shuffle backwards.'

She climbed on awkwardly and then

gripped the back handle tightly.

'Are you comfortable?' he asked, as the bike sank under his weight.

It took all the strength her arms could muster to stop sliding towards him.

'Mmm,' she murmured.

'Tonight went well,' he said as he clipped his helmet strap under his chin.

'Do you think so?'

'Don't you?' He turned slightly to look at her, his head comically large under his helmet.

'We only got eight people to sign up. That's a very low percentage.'

'Those are the people who are actively going to help us, but mostly people are against the idea. Perhaps you didn't follow that part of the debate. Some of the older residents have strong local accents even I struggle to understand. Right, hold on tight, I'm going to rock the bike to release the kick stand.'

She squealed as the bike rocked precariously under her. She didn't hear him laugh but his shoulders shook so she knew he was finding her terror amusing.

If she wasn't so frightened, she'd think of a way to get him back.

Without warning he started the bike and they were off. For a few terrifying seconds the world whizzed past and Annie clung to the bar behind her. Her palms felt slick and she worried that they would slip off the rail. They leaped over speed bumps and Annie was airborne before she landed back on the seat with a thud.

'It's plain sailing from here,' Giovanni shouted. 'No more speed bumps to worry about.'

'I'm worried my hands are going to let go of the bar,' she shouted back.

'They aren't — but if you're worried, you can hold onto me instead.'

Annie gritted her teeth and refused to move. 'I don't bite,' shouted Giovanni over the whistling of the wind.

Giovanni slowed at a junction and Annie risked releasing her tight grip on the bar. She flung her arms around Giovanni as he sped off again.

With her nose pressed against his

jacket she could smell his unique smell, lemon mixed with the scent of outdoors. She felt him laugh as they turned a corner and tightened her grip.

Even though it was winter he was only wearing a light jacket, and as the next mile flew past Annie relaxed enough to notice how firm his chest was. It was a relief when they pulled up outside the cottage and she could let go of him.

'How did you find it?' he asked.

'Terrifying.'

She was close enough to see the fine lines around his eyes crinkle with his smile. She'd never seen him so amused. It was like meeting a completely different man.

'Will you try it again for yourself?' he asked, obviously not so entranced with her face as she was with his.

'Um...'

'I will come down early tomorrow. We will have a go and then walk up to the castle to get started on the painting.'

Annie had forgotten he'd offered to come and help her out this weekend.

Before she could tell him it wasn't necessary — she didn't know how much of him she could take before she started acting like the gaggle of women who'd surrounded him earlier — he'd jumped off the bike and was waving goodbye.

14

'I thought,' said Giovanni by way of a greeting the following morning, 'that we could go the long way round to the castello. That way you could get some practice on the roads.'

'I'm not going anywhere without breakfast,' Annie said, hoping to put off the inevitable. 'Have you eaten?'

'I thought we could stop in town and eat.'

'I've got bacon cooking. Would you like a sandwich?' she offered.

'Yeah, it smells good, so thanks,' he said as he followed her into the cottage.

He seemed extra large in the small space. He'd also reverted to his usual serious demeanour and was looking at the trinkets Tilly and she had put around the place to make it more homely.

'Is this your daughter?' he asked, picking up a photograph frame.

'Yes, that's Molly,' she said.

He smiled slightly and put the frame down. He pulled out a chair at the dining table and sat down. Annie cut two crusty rolls and spread them with butter, the bacon hissing and spitting in the pan next to her.

'Would you like a coffee with it?' she asked.

'Yes — I can make it.'

'No, you sit down. There's not enough room for the two of us in this kitchen.'

She'd become used to the thick, dark coffee preferred by the Italians and she poured one for herself as well as for him.

'Thank you,' he said, when she placed the plate and cup in front of him.

They ate in silence. Annie was glad. She hated having to make conversation before she'd finished eating in the morning. She didn't feel entirely awake before she'd had her last mouthful.

'That's enough procrastinating,' he said as he brushed crumbs onto his plate. 'It's time for you to get onto the bike.'

'Why don't we walk up this morning?' she suggested.

'Because we're going by bike,' he insisted, his lips twitching as he watched her reaction.

He picked up her helmet, which she'd left on the settee last night, and handed it to her.

'Try riding it without me first,' he suggested when they were outside.

She clambered on, not feeling in the least bit graceful, and settled herself behind the handlebars.

'Remember you need to release the kick stand first, then turn the key and off you go.'

Annie tried to imitate the strange rocking motion Giovanni had done last night but all that happened was that Giovanni stifled a laugh.

'You need to give it more force,' he suggested, a hint of laughter creeping into his voice.

She tried again and released the stand. 'Well done. Now turn this here and ...'

Annie felt the bike surge beneath her and then she was flying down the road. She felt a thrill race through her.

'I'm doing it!' she shouted. 'How do I stop it?'

'Stop twisting the accelerator and pull the brakes,' he shouted as he ran alongside her.

'How can you be running at the same speed as me? I'm flying along.'

Giovanni stopped running as he burst out laughing. Annie brought the moped to a standstill and climbed off as she waited for him to stop sniggering.

'You were not going as fast as perhaps it felt,' he said, when he had pulled himself together.

'How do you turn it around?' she asked with as much dignity as she could muster.

'There's no need to turn around. We'll go into town and up to the castle this way,' he said.

'Don't you think I need just a little more practice before I'm unleashed onto the roads?'

The skin around Giovanni's eyes crinkled as he grinned at her. She crossed her arms, she was still a little cross with him for laughing so heartily but it was hard to hold onto the feeling when he turned that megawatt smile on her. Being in a relationship with him must be a nightmare. All he'd have to do was smile and he'd win every argument.

'No, that's really all there is to it,' he said. 'I'm sure people walking can get out of your way if you start coming towards them. Besides, I can always take over if you need me to.'

'Are you going to run alongside for the whole way?'

He grinned, 'No, I'm going on the back.'

Without waiting for her to protest he climbed onto the passenger seat and waited for her to get on as well.

She climbed onto the seat and started the moped back up again. She could feel the weight of him behind her but he didn't touch her and she was glad. She could do without the distraction.

She gripped the handlebars tightly and began to drive towards the town. After a mile she could feel him shaking with repressed mirth.

'What's so funny?' she shouted over her shoulder.

'I think we've just been overtaken by a snail,' he said in her ear.

She shivered as his breath whispered along her skin.

'I feel like we're going at about ninety kilometres an hour,' she yelled.

'It's more like ninety kilometres a year.'

'Do you want to get off and walk?'

'It would be quicker but, no, I'm enjoying myself too much.'

She ignored him and went back to concentrating on the road. Her palms were slick with sweat by the time they reached the castello but her heart was racing with joy.

'I did it,' she said, leaping off the bike.

'Yeah, you did.' Giovanni was grinning at her.

'You were amazing.'

'Yes, I really was.'

Energy was coursing through her. She could do anything today. If she could ride a moped, she could paint two bedroom ceilings and still have time left over to paint walls. The sky was the limit. She unlocked the castle entrance and stepped shyly into the lobby. It still took her breath away with its elegant simplicity and she wanted Giovanni to be impressed. If she could achieve this look throughout the hotel, then it was going to be a triumph, even if she did say so herself.

'Wow,' he said, looking around the room. 'Every time I come in here it's taken another amazing leap forward.'

She smiled, pleased with his reaction and headed off to the storeroom. This room would eventually house linen but was now stocked with paint. It was cramped and uncomfortable and only one person could fit in comfortably.

'Do you think you could take that?' she said, holding out a ladder to him as he stood by the door.

'Sure. Shall I take the other one too?'
'Can you manage both?'
'Sure. I work on a farm, remember.

Lifting things is what I do.'

She turned away from the sight of him lifting the ladders over one shoulder. It really wouldn't do to keep ogling his muscles even if they did look delicious under his T-shirt.

She set Giovanni up in a room opposite the one she was working in. They could still talk, but they weren't in close proximity. This way she wouldn't keep getting wafts of his delicious scent or get distracted by his strength.

'Are you sure you want to do this?' she asked. 'I'm sure,' he said, bending down to lever the lid off a paint pot.

'OK, I'm across the hall if you need anything.'

He nodded but didn't look at her as he started to sort through the paint brushes she'd left out.

She flicked the radio on before climbing up her own ladder. She'd been listening to an Italian station to try and pick up more of the language. She could now understand most of what was being said unless an advert came on — then the speech was so fast she couldn't keep up.

A song came on and Giovanni began to sing along. Annie sniggered. He did not have a good singing voice.

'Are you laughing at me?' he called across. 'Of course not,' she said, her voice trembling with suppressed mirth.

He sang louder. She laughed out loud and heard his answering chuckle.

Later they leaned against the castle walls to eat the food Annie had prepared. A brisk wind pushed at the large, grey clouds making bursts of sunshine pierce through every now and then. Annie loved the way the sun picked out sparkles in the sea and she watched contentedly, not feeling the need to make conversation.

'You're covered in paint,' he commented.

'So are you,' she said smiling.

Flecks of white emulsion covered his face and were caught in the hair on his forearms.

Slowly, almost imperceptibly his face

moved towards hers. For a heartbeat she thought he was going to kiss her and then he straightened.

'Are you expecting anyone?' he asked.

'What?' she said stupidly.

'I can hear a car. Is Tilly due back today?'

It took Annie a moment to get back to the present.

'She's not due back until Monday and I'm not expecting any deliveries today.'

Giovanni pulled Annie behind an archway as two dark cars swept up the hillside and stopped metres away from the castle entrance.

'What's going on?' whispered Annie.

'Global Hotel,' answered Giovanni succinctly.

'Are you sure?'

'No, but look who it is.'

Annie peered out from behind a column and saw the man she knew to be the town planner, Lorenzo Moretti, step out of a car wearing his signature yellow suit.

'Can you tell what they are saying?'

she asked. Giovanni held up a finger and nodded brusquely. Gradually the men moved away and Giovanni let her go. She missed the warmth and security of his arms immediately.

'The men in suits were asking the town planner, Signor Moretti, if they should be worried about the local opposition to their hotel. The town planner dismissed us as crazy people.'

Annie gasped. 'How dare he? I'm going to speak to him now.'

'What? No, Annie, wait —'

Giovanni's fingers grazed her arm as she stormed out of their hiding place and marched down the hill towards the group of men. She was not going to lie down and let herself be walked all over again. The town planner was going to regret the day he ever thought to dismiss Annie Smith.

15

Giovanni watched Annie storm down the hill towards the group of men who were unaware they were about to be shouted at by a wild woman. He should have told her that her face was streaked with blobs of paint and that there was a large clump of it in her hair. In his defence, he hadn't expected her to fly down the hill like a scruffy avenging angel.

He'd been content to talk with a woman not bothered about her appearance. After working in modelling for so long, she was a breath of fresh air. Who knows what he'd have done if the men hadn't arrived when they did? He'd wanted to kiss her and it had looked as if she wanted the kiss too.

Despite the seriousness of the situation, he couldn't help but smile as Annie tapped the town planner on his shoulder. His look of horror as he turned and took in Annie's furious paint-splattered expression was priceless.

Giovanni supposed he should go and help Annie. She might get into one of her funny muddles over the language, which would undermine her argument and make her feel foolish.

He made his way slowly down towards the group and watched as the town planner tried to speak over Annie's angry protestations.

She was so different from the woman he'd met in September. Then she'd been buttoned up and subdued; now she was a whirling dervish with her arms flying everywhere as she made her point. He could watch her for hours, which was a problem.

These strange urges to spend as much time with Annie as possible had to be quashed — especially now he knew she was nothing like his ex-wife. Where Ashley had been self-centred, Annie never seemed to think about herself at all. The last thing he needed to do was fall for her, though. There was no guarantee she would stay in Italy for long. She obviously adored her daughter and would want to live near her.

If it was just him, he would risk his heart being broken again — but he had to think of Serena. She didn't deserve another woman in her life, leaving her, and so he had to get rid of this unwanted attraction.

The problem was, his mind thought one thing and his body made him do something entirely different.

Giovanni caught up with Annie as the group of men were returning to the cars.

'Buon pomerriggio, Giovanni. Do you know this lady?' asked the town planner.

Next to him Annie made a snort of disgust and tightly folded her arms across her chest.

'This is Annie. She and her aunt own Castello di Giacobbella,' Giovanni told him.

'Perhaps you could tell her that I object to being accused of being a liar and whatever else she was trying to say in her inadequate Italian.'

'You can tell me yourself,' said Annie in perfect Italian. 'I'm not blind.'

'You mean deaf,' said Giovanni, trying not to smile. He really didn't want to undermine her, especially in front of this slimy toad, but he did find her very amusing when she got her words mixed up.

'That too.'

Lorenzo pulled himself up to his full height, which just about reached Annie's shoulders and said, 'You have been very rude, signora. Not to mention aggressive. I wouldn't be surprised if my colleagues filed a complaint against your behaviour.'

'With whom will they file this complaint?' demanded Annie in English. She shook her head and began again in Italian. 'I don't work for those men and I haven't committed a crime. No one can file a complaint. And how are they colleagues? You work for the council and they work for Global Hotel. Is Global Hotel giving you money? Is that why you are allowing this... this...' she paused as she tried to find the right word, '... abomination to be built?'

The town planner was going an interesting shade of red and a vein was pulsing wildly at the base of his throat.

'Is it true, then?' asked Giovanni. 'You are giving the go-ahead for a hotel development to be built here?'

'Nothing has been decided yet,' said Lorenzo officiously. 'Global Hotel is exploring a number of sites all over the island. This is one of the places they are interested in.'

'What other sites?' demanded Annie, her fists clenched tightly by her sides.

'Rest assured,' said the town planner directly to Giovanni as if Annie hadn't spoken, 'everyone shall be notified when they reach their final decision and an application has been made.'

The town planner stormed off to his car. Annie sniggered as he stumbled over a stone and he turned to glare at her. She didn't try to hide her reaction and Giovanni felt a surge of pride at her refusal to back down.

It wasn't until the cars carrying the business men disappeared over the brow of the hill that Annie turned to look at him. Her eyes were shining with unshed tears.

'They are going to build here, aren't they?' she said hoarsely. 'I mean, if they weren't going to he would have said as much and I don't believe there are other sites they're considering. It's going to destroy the area. I can't bear it.'

She flung herself at Giovanni. He caught her as she threw her arms around him and buried her head in his chest. Her whole body trembled and he held her tightly.

She stayed in his arms for a few blissful minutes before pushing against his chest and pulling away. He let go of her reluctantly.

'I'm sorry. I didn't mean to use you as a human tissue,' she said, attempting a smile.

'It's fine,' he said.

It was more than fine. He enjoyed having her in his arms way more than he should.

'Right,' she said, pulling herself upright. 'What are we going to do about this travesty?'

Giovanni knew he should be concentrating on Global Hotel but his body was aching to hold her again and his mind was a few steps behind.

He cleared his throat and rubbed his chin.

'I'll ring the others who have agreed to help,' he said. 'We don't have to fight this alone.'

'Yes, you're right.' She nodded. 'Perhaps we can meet up this evening.'

'Good idea,' he said. 'It will have to start after I've collected Serena from my parents. Perhaps around seven?'

He tried to ignore the delight flooding through his body at the thought of spending another evening with Annie.

Thank you,' she whispered. 'I'm so glad you're on my side.'

She reached across and squeezed his hand before quickly dropping it and turning to walk back up to the castle.

He let out a long breath and then slowly followed her.

16

Giovanni's kitchen was full of people. Annie sat next to Greta and helped herself to another bowl of Carlotta's delicious soup. She'd missed what it was called, the Italian name was too quick for her, but she found its creamy texture soothing to her taut stomach.

'Would you like some more, too?' she asked Greta, who was sitting next to her.

'Yes, please.' Greta handed over her bowl. 'I can't get enough of Carlotta's cooking.'

Annie ladled another helping of soup into her friend's bowl and passed it over to her.

'When will things start happening?' she asked. 'We must take care of the formalities first, this is the way things are done in Italy,' said Greta.

'Have patience.'

Annie slumped back in her seat, disappointed.

They'd all been here for at least an hour and nothing had been said about Global Hotel. There had been a lot of talk about families and people Annie didn't know, and she was starting to wish she'd stayed at the cottage and mapped out her own plan of action.

She'd rung Tilly not long after Lorenzo and the other goons had driven off. Tilly felt just as frantic about the development as Annie did, but she was stuck on the other side of the island in the midst of sales negotiations that seemed never-ending and she didn't know when she would be back.

'None of Giovanni's fan club has turned up,' muttered Greta, scanning the room and checking out the guests while slurping up her soup.

Annie felt her cheeks warm and leaned closer to her soup, hoping any redness would be explained away by the heat coming off it. She'd already noticed that none of the women who'd been fawning over Giovanni at the last meeting were here. She'd been glad and then horrified.

184

Fancying him was one thing — but under no circumstances must she develop feelings for the man, or harbour any hope that there could be more between them than friendship.

There were so many reasons it was a bad idea. She'd taken a moment to list them to herself — a relationship with someone who lived in a different country was destined for heartbreak; and even if it was possible Giovanni was too good-looking to consider her as a potential girlfriend. He was used to being surrounded by supermodels. She needed to get her emotions under control, fast.

A small hand tugged on her sleeve. 'Annie,' said a small voice.

Annie looked down to find Serena next to her holding up a crumpled piece of paper.

Annie took it gently. 'How lovely,' she said in Italian. 'What have you made?'

Serena gabbled something in response and Annie looked to Greta for help.

'It's a duck. Un'anatra,' said her friend.

'It's a beautiful duck,' Annie said and she was rewarded with a dazzling smile.

'For you,' said Serena happily.

'Thank you. I shall treasure it. Would you like to play with it for now?'

Serena nodded and took Annie by surprise by clambering up onto her lap and placing the duck on the table in front of them both, making quacking noises as she moved it around.

It had been so long since a small child had sat on Annie's lap that she'd forgotten how bony their bottoms could be. She adjusted the girl's weight and resisted the urge to start playing with the thick black curls that were tickling her nose.

'You've made a friend,' said Greta, grinning. 'She is very lovely,' said Annie, switching to English so that Serena couldn't understand what she was saying.

'Yes, she's going to be a stunner when she grows up — but with both her parents that's hardly surprising.' Greta lowered her voice and moved closer. 'It doesn't look as if her mum is here. Do you know what's happened to her?'

'No idea,' said Annie concentrating very hard on the back of Serena's head.

She felt Greta watching her for a moment.

'I don't believe you,' said Greta. 'But I won't press you because that would be mean.'

Annie felt her shoulders relax. She didn't like keeping things from her friend but this wasn't her secret to reveal.

'Rumour has it,' said Greta, a laugh creeping into her voice, 'that you were seen earlier today travelling towards the castello on a moped belonging to our gorgeous host and that he was on it with you.'

'It's true,' said Annie briskly. 'He's lent me his moped to get around on and he was teaching me how to ride it. It was good fun.'

'I'm sure it was, with that hunk of a man wrapped around you.'

'He was holding the handlebar at the back, not on to me,' said Annie, still refusing to look at Greta. 'Ah, look — something is about to happen.'

Giovanni was standing and trying to quieten everyone down and Annie was grateful for the diversion. It was one thing to have a secret crush on Giovanni, quite another if anyone found out.

'Silenzio!' shouted Greta. The room quieted.

'Thanks, Greta,' Giovanni said and Greta pouted with pleasure.

Annie rolled her eyes. Perhaps Greta wasn't cottoning on to Annie's secret crush after all. She probably assumed that all women crushed on Giovanni a little bit, which was depressingly true and yet another reason why she shouldn't.

'Thank you all for coming tonight,' Giovanni continued. 'It looks like we are right to be concerned about Global Hotel's plans. They were seen today looking at the area of land between Castello di Giacobbella and the beach.

'Although nothing official has been declared yet I do believe this is strong enough evidence that they are planning

188

something for that area.

'I also believe that a hotel complex here will change the area completely and will have a devastating impact on the local wildlife and will destroy our local beach, which will become flooded with tourists. Any ideas you may have on how we can stop them would be gratefully appreciated.'

'Why don't we club together buy the land?' called out a man whose dark brown, bald head reminded Annie strongly of a nut.

'OK, that's one suggestion. Thank you, Pedro,' said Giovanni, making a note. 'We offer to buy the land from the council.'

'It will be very expensive,' said Carlotta.

Giovanni nodded. 'We'd have to do some fundraising and I'm not sure how much time we have, but it's a good idea and one we'll need to look into in more depth.'

Soon suggestions were flying around the table, ranging from the ridiculous —

chase the developers out of town, to the more sensible — arranging petitions and staging protests.

The evening wore on. Sometimes Annie understood what was being said, sometimes she didn't. The exchanges often seemed heated but then laughter would break out and Annie assumed it was just their way of talking.

Serena started to become heavy in her lap and after a while her small head flopped backwards into Annie's chest. She caught Giovanni's eye and gestured that she would carry Serena upstairs to bed. He nodded and Annie got slowly to her feet, making sure not to jolt the sleeping child awake.

She managed to slide Serena into bed without waking her, and took a moment to gaze at her.

Night-time had been one of Annie's favourite parenting moments. When Molly was soft with sleep and she could take a moment to study her features, knowing she was safe for a few hours before she woke and started tearing round again.

She backed away from the bed and made it to the door before a sleepy voice called out, 'Libro.'

Serena's eyes were half-open, but she was clutching a book in her tiny hands.

Annie made her way back to the bed and took the book from her. Glancing at the pages, she realised she hadn't a hope in reading the story.

'How about I tell you a new story instead?' she said softly.

The little girl nodded and scooted over on the bed so that Annie could sit down, resting her head on Annie's lap when she did so.

A little thump of love pounded in Annie's heart and she tried to rub it away. Loving someone else's daughter would only end in pain. It wasn't as if she could make Serena hers. But maybe she was mistaking the sensation she'd felt. She had eaten a lot of Carlotta's creamy soup, so perhaps it was only a bit of heartburn.

She began a story she'd made up for Molly when she was younger involving a young boy and girl who travelled the world in search of adventure.

In the warmth and comfort of the room, Annie's own eyelids began to feel heavy and very slowly the world went black around her.

★ ★ ★

Annie's eyelids flickered open. She sighed — she really didn't want to get up to go and start painting again. Her muscles ached and she was so bored of it. She closed her eyes again and rolled over. There would be time enough later.

Sleep tugged at her but something was niggling at her consciousness. She sat bolt upright.

She wasn't in her bedroom at the cottage. She threw back the covers. She was fully dressed — but where was she? The last thing she remembered was... Oh, she must still be at Giovanni's house — but she'd been moved from Serena's bed and into this one. How incredible that she hadn't woken up. She wasn't normally a heavy sleeper.

She pulled her phone out of her pocket to check the time, but it was dead. It had to be early; she never slept late, and she'd had an earlier night than usual.

She slid out of bed and padded to the doorway. The house was silent. She'd creep downstairs and leave a note thanking Giovanni for letting her stay, as well as apologising for falling asleep in his daughter's bed. All she had to do was find her shoes and then she could make her escape.

Slowly Annie opened the door. She was in a bedroom further down the hallway than she'd been before. She'd have to tiptoe past Giovanni's and Serena's bedrooms without waking them but that was no problem. Molly had been a very light sleeper when she was a baby, and she'd mastered the art of moving quietly.

She moved into the hallway and stopped. There was no movement. She

could get away without the embarrassment of having to see Giovanni.

She moved softly along the corridor
and breathed a sigh of relief as she got
past Serena's room without disturbing
the little girl.

She was almost confident by the time
she reached the stairs, and she slipped
down them quickly and quietly.

There were a pile of shoes by the front
door that didn't look as if they'd been left
in any order at all. Her fingers itched to
put the matching pairs together but she
refused to give into the urge. She needed
to find hers and get out before Giovanni
awoke.

She spotted her boots towards the
back of the pile and leaned over to pick
them up. As she stooped, a pair of arms
flung themselves around her legs and she
stumbled, knocking her head against the
wall.

'Are you OK?' asked a deep voice from
behind her. 'I'm sorry Serena attacked you
but she has been excitedly waiting for you
to wake up for a couple of hours now.'

194

'A couple of hours,' Annie repeated. She righted herself and rubbed her head. It was a bit sore, but not too bad. 'What time is it?'

Giovanni glanced at his watch. 'It's coming up to ten.'

'Ten! Are you sure? How can I have slept for so long? I need to get back to the castle. I've got so much to do.'

Annie made another grab for her boots. This time she managed to get them without being knocked off her feet.

'Surely you can take a little time off. Serena has been hoping you will come for our Sunday walk with us. We always go down to the beach to see if we can spot dragons. So far we've not been successful, but maybe today's the day. You wouldn't want to miss that, would you?'

Annie made the mistake of looking down into Serena's large, hopeful eyes.

'I can fill you in on what was decided last night,' Giovanni added.

'OK — let me go home and change

and I'll come with you for a walk,' said Annie reluctantly.

This was not going to help her resolve to keep her heart safe from these two.

17

Half an hour later, Giovanni and Annie followed a running Serena through the straight lines of gnarled olive trees that made up the majority of Giovanni's farm. Annie was braving it in only a thin T-shirt with her jeans. The March sun was warming her arms and reminding her that summer was only around the corner.

'I'm sorry I fell asleep during the meeting last night,' she said.

Giovanni laughed. 'You were exhausted and the meeting must have been hard for you to follow. Thank you for taking care of Serena. She has been talking non-stop about your imaginary heroes since she woke up this morning.'

Annie didn't want to talk about Serena. It seemed the little girl was as taken with Annie as Annie was with her — but that was a bad thing. She was going to leave soon, and then Serena would have another woman she cared about leaving. Best if Annie kept her distance from today.

'I did get a bit confused during the meeting,' she said. 'What was decided?'

'Pedro, the guy who was getting a bit hot under the collar...'

'I know the one. I thought he looked like a nut.' Giovanni laughed. 'I guess he does with his shiny, dark head. He's a designer and he's going to put together a leaflet outlining why we think Global Hotel's development will be a bad idea for the town. We're all going to take some and post them in at every address in Vescovina and the houses in the surrounding countryside. We're hoping to follow that up with asking people to sign a petition once they've had time to read about our concerns.

'There's also been the suggestion of us pooling our money and buying the land but I can't see that happening. Most of the people in the meeting don't have any spare money. It's not as if owning a share of the land will ever give them any profit.'

'I will ask Tilly if she can put money towards it. I guess it will depend on how much she has sunk into her two latest projects.'

Giovanni nodded thoughtfully. 'I may be able to donate some money but I don't have a great deal left after agreeing to buy your Aunt Tilly's land from her. She drives a hard bargain.'

Annie grinned. 'I told you she was a canny businesswoman.'

'Yeah, she is. Although don't tell her, but I think I'm getting a bargain.'

Annie laughed, 'It's too late to tell her now anyway. When I spoke to Tilly yesterday she said you were nearly at completion stage.'

'Yes, I will own the land in a week or two.'

'Does that mean you will be very busy preparing the land, or whatever it is that you do?'

'I will be busy, yes. But don't worry. I will still have time to fight Global Hotel.'

Annie nodded, relieved. If Giovanni was going to be busy, then it meant less time for them to spend together and before too long she would be heading back to Britain. The longer she spent away from him, the more likely her heart would stay safe from falling in love.

'I haven't been down to the beach yet,' confessed Annie as they entered the pine forest that bordered the beach for a couple of miles.

'Really?' said Giovanni, surprised. 'I guess you haven't been here during the warmer months when coming to the beach is a daily ritual for most Vescovinians.'

Annie wrinkled her nose. What did people find to do at the beach every day? She preferred it in winter when she could stride across the sand unimpeded by others. Summertime at the coast was a nightmare of overcrowding and gritty sandwiches.

'I can see you don't believe me,' said Giovanni.

'It's not that, I just don't understand why you would want to come to the beach every day.'

'To lie in the sun and to talk to friends. Some of the older folk sit in the shade of the trees and play chess. It's to socialise. Is that not something you do in Britain?'

'The sand at the beach closest to me is a bit coarse. I can't really imagine lying on it for any length of time. I guess we took the children to beaches when they were growing up, but I remember mostly struggling with a windbreak and huddling in thick jumpers to keep warm.'

'I think you will find this very different.' A faint smile touched the edge of his lips.

Serena darted back to join them.

'Come, Annie, come,' she said tugging Annie's hand and dragging her forward through the last of the pine trees and out onto a wide expanse of soft, white sand.

The bay was smaller than she'd imagined with the sand curving gently around and ending at an outcrop of pale stones that jutted out into the aquamarine sea.

'Oh my,' said Annie. 'It's beautiful... It's like something you'd see in the movies. I can't believe we're the only ones here to enjoy it.'

Giovanni smiled. Serena raced onto the beach and started scuffing the sand with her boots.

'If you climb over those rocks,' said Giovanni, pointing to the outcrop, 'you'll come to the next beach along, which is the nearest one to your hotel. Although this is a more beautiful spot it's less popular, even in the summertime, because it's harder to get to.'

'Is there a path?'

'There is more than one way to get here, but unless you come through my land, every other way involves quite a steep climb. It's all right on the way down to the beach, but people don't enjoy a long walk after an afternoon relaxing.

'It's one of the reasons I'm so worried about the development. If tourists think they can trample over my land to get to the beach, then they could damage the trees. I've also heard from other farmers living near developments and you wouldn't believe how many people think it's fine to pick fruit. They don't seem to realise it's theft.' He shrugged and smiled and something strange twanged in Annie's chest. She looked around for something to talk about.

'How about going over those rocks? Are they dangerous?'

'No, but it takes a while. We can do it now if you like. Serena enjoys it. Then we can walk back through the ruins you are so fond of.'

'I can manage on my own if you want to get back,' Annie suggested.

She half-hoped he would take her up on the offer. The other half yearned to spend the day with him and his beautiful daughter.

'It's not a problem for us to come with you. We've no other plans today. Besides, imagine you get stuck up there? I'd be in trouble with Carlotta if I abandoned her friend. Plus, I imagine Tilly would be reluctant to sell me the land if she thought I'd lost her niece.'

Annie laughed and a little thrill ran through her, which was ridiculous. He wasn't staying with her because he cared about her safety but because he felt obliged.

'If Global Hotel get their way, do you think tourists will come to this beach as well — or is the path really that bad?' Annie asked.

'With the money at Global Hotel's disposal I'm sure they could afford to add steps to make it safer and easier, or maybe run golf buggies back and forth for the guests. I think I read online that they do that at some of their other hotels.'

Annie stared at the track along the edge of the pine trees and tried to imagine it lined with golf carts waiting for tourists to finish their day at the beach. The tranquillity, which made this place special, would be destroyed.

She turned and walked to the shoreline. The waves made a gentle whoosh as they lapped against the sand. She'd never understood the attraction of the beach before but standing here, in paradise, she finally did. This was a slice of serenity that soothed the soul.

'Every time I hear something ab out Global Hotel it gets worse,' she said. 'How can the council even think for a second that this big hotel complex is a good idea? Don't they see that they would be spoiling the area for themselves as well as everyone else? What possesses someone to ignore their common sense like this?'

'Money,' said Giovanni succinctly. He came to stand by her and they watched a little sailing boat bobbing about on the gentle waves far out to sea.

'Shall we…?' he said, when it had sailed out of sight, and she nodded.

Giovanni turned and spoke rapidly to Serena in Italian. Annie caught enough to understand that they were going to help the English lady over the rocks. Serena started to giggle.

'She thinks you're clumsy, I'm afraid,' said Giovanni with a grin.

'What's given her that idea?' Annie protested. 'I may have told her how I was attacked by a crazy English woman on the first day we met. I may have also exaggerated the situation to get a few laughs.'

'Well,' said Annie in mock anger, 'I'll just have to prove that I am all that is lithe and graceful.'

She marched purposefully over to the rocks and started to clamber up the side. She hauled herself up the first section easily. This was going to be easy. Beside her Serena scrambled up the edge like a mountain goat, her little legs flashing past in a blur. Annie was confident she would join her up at the top pretty quickly.

She stretched and used both her arms to pull herself up higher. She managed to find a foothold for her left leg, although it was slightly uncomfortable at almost ninety degrees to her body. Her other leg was left dangling.

'I think I might be stuck,' she called out after a few minutes of waving her leg about.

There was no response.

She peered under her right arm and saw that Giovanni was still standing on the sand, doubled up with silent laughter.

'You're not helping,' she said as the desire to laugh coursed through her, weakening her arms.

'Sorry,' he wheezed. 'I wasn't sure what lithe meant in Italian but now I know it has a similar meaning to clumsy.' She giggled.

'Ahh — I need you to stop making fun at my expense and help,' she said, feeling her grip on the rocks slip.

She didn't have far to go if she fell, but she would prefer not to find out if the short distance would hurt or not.

Above her Serena was giggling with delight. 'Is she safe up there?' Annie asked, afraid to twist her head to look.

'She's sitting down on a flat surface so she'll be fine. It's you I need to worry about. Here let me help you find somewhere to put this foot.'

Giovanni's hand gripped her right ankle. 'How about here?'

'Ahh — no, that's worse. I'm not that bendy.'

Giovanni snorted with laughter but

didn't comment.

'I'm not sure I can hold on for much longer.' Giovanni's laughter vibrated against her leg.

'OK, I'm going to come up and join you.'

'How will that help?'

'I'll be able to catch you if you fall.'

'I'm quite heavy. I don't think you'll be able to hold us both to the cliff.'

'It's a large rock, Annie. And I'm a farmer, remember. I spend my days lifting cows so I'm sure I can manage one tiny woman.'

'You're a fruit farmer, so don't give me that rubbish about cows. There's very little weight in an olive — and I'm not tiny.'

He drew level with her. 'You're smaller than me.'

'Not by that much and ... what are you doing?'

Giovanni's arm had come round her waist and he was pulling her towards him.

'I'm going to get you up to the top.

Relax.'

Annie couldn't relax. She was now pinned between Giovanni and the rock face. She could feel his breath whisper across the nape of her neck and her skin tingled in response.

Gently he took one of her hands in his strong, warm one and placed it on a ledge not far from her head.

'I wouldn't stretch much further than that in any one move,' he said. 'Otherwise you might find yourself spread-eagled again and as much as Serena and I enjoyed the sight, I don't think you did.'

'Mmm,' she murmured.

She was finding it very difficult to concentrate on climbing when she could feel the buckle of his jeans belt through her flimsy T-shirt. Her breathing was coming in short puffs. She had to get away from him, and quickly.

She placed her other hand above her and said, 'You can let go now.'

'There's not really anywhere for me to go. You keep going up and I'll stay here.'

She scrambled up and away from him

as quickly as she could manage. It didn't take her long to reach the top, which was indeed flat. She sat next to Serena on the hard rock and waited for Giovanni to join them. Serena had stopped laughing at her and had picked up a pebble with which she was drawing stick men on the rock.

Giovanni was grinning as he pulled himself up onto the top. When she saw his wide smile Serena's little body collapsed against Annie in peals of laughter again. Annie slipped her arm around Serena's shoulder and she snuggled closer, snorting gleefully.

'Was it really that funny?' asked Annie.

'Ah, you know children, they love a bit of slapstick. I hope you don't mind her laughing so much. I know I should tell her not to laugh at you but she's been so sad since Ashley left that I don't want to stop her.'

Annie looked at Giovanni crouched low on the rock. He was looking at his daughter, the love he felt for her evident in every line of his body.

'Of course I don't mind. What sort of a monster would I be if I didn't like to hear a child's laughter?'

Giovanni glanced at her and then looked away. 'Ashley didn't like to be laughed at,' he confessed in English. 'Not even by Serena.'

Annie huffed. 'I didn't think my opinion of her could get much lower but you've just proved that it's possible. What did you see in her?'

Giovanni smiled. 'She was very beautiful. She still is.' Annie's hands clenched involuntarily. 'I was flattered that she was interested in me but it wasn't long after we married that I realised she was more into the way we looked together than she was into me as a person. I was an accessory and she was getting as bored of me as she would an out-of-season handbag. I was thinking of taking the big step of ending the marriage. I knew it would upset my parents, but I was so unhappy. Then she announced she was pregnant. I hoped the baby would bring us together but obviously that never happens to anyone and I was a fool to think we could be different.'

'You weren't a fool — she was.'

Giovanni looked at her and a slow smile broke out across his face.

'Thank you. Does this mean you no longer think of me as Carlotta's obnoxious older brother?'

Heat swept across her face.

'I never thought you were obnoxious.' Giovanni let out a bark of laughter.

'I thought you were grumpy and surly but not obnoxious,' Annie smiled despite the fact that her brain was screaming at her to stop this flirting. It was dangerous ... and was making Annie's insides squirm with pleasure.

'You were right. I was very rude to you when you first arrived. I thought you were part of Global Hotel's plans and then I thought you had abandoned your child, just like Ashley, to follow your own dreams. I'm sorry for the way I acted.'

Annie hadn't expected Giovanni to admit he hadn't been nice to her when she'd arrived. Her heart beat faster as

Giovanni simply looked at her, a light smile playing around his lips.

'Papà,' said Serena, holding out a rock for her father to see.

Annie jumped. She had forgotten all about the little girl who was curled up against her.

'We really must get going,' she said abruptly.

Whatever was going on here had to stop. She'd already told herself so many times that Giovanni was out of bounds, so what was she doing staring into his eyes like a lovesick teenager?

'OK,' said Giovanni, not commenting on her sudden change of mood. 'It's a fairly flat walk for about fifty metres and then we have to climb down on the other side.

Annie stood up, marched ahead and soon reached the edge of the rocky out-crop. From this point she could see the long, wide bay she could glimpse from the castello's windows. The sand and sea were as glorious as the secluded cove but this beach had a completely different feel.

Annie could imagine young families playing together while groups of teenagers sat around chatting on the soft sand... while the little cove behind her was for young lovers.

Without waiting for Giovanni to catch up, she jumped down. Her knees reverberated with the impact but she remained standing.

'Are you all right?' Giovanni called from high above her.

'I'm fine. Thanks so much for today. I've loved seeing the beaches but I've just realised the time and I need to get going.'

'Oh... don't you...?'

'No, I'm sorry. Time really is of the essence. Ciao, Serena. Bye, Giovanni. I'll see you around.' She turned and walked briskly along the beach, hoping that Giovanni hadn't noticed she wasn't wearing a watch.

18

Giovanni laughed and clapped as Serena and Sofia finished a little dance they'd put on for his benefit. Sofia was a much nicer teenager than he'd ever been, and seemed to enjoy spending time with her cousin who was so much younger than her. Serena adored her for it and followed her everywhere.

'Go to the kitchen, Papà, we need to practise another dance,' demanded Serena.

Giovanni glanced at Sofia. If she needed rescuing, he would take Serena away with him, but the older girl only nodded and smiled at him.

'OK, I'll look forward to seeing it later,' he said and made his way back to his sister's kitchen. There was a smell of freshly baked bread and something sweet he couldn't identify. To his delight, the kitchen table was covered in small, golden-topped loaves. He reached for one but Carlotta's hand slapped his away.

'That's for the shop,' she admonished him. Giovanni's stomach rumbled in protest.

'I'll pay you for it,' he said, reaching out to tear off a piece. Carlotta moved it out of his reach.

'But then I'd have nothing to sell and what sort of a shopkeeper would that make me?'

'What sort of a sister would see her brother starve?' he countered.

'The one who's got food in the fridge he can eat,' she said, giving him a plate and nudging him away from the table.

'You are amazing,' said Giovanni, pulling open the door and helping himself to some of the cheeses and hams that were stuffed in there.

His sister let him pile up a huge plate of food, which should have made him suspect something was up. But he was so hungry he didn't think anything of it until she said, 'What's going on between you and Annie?'

He choked on an olive. 'What do you

mean?'

'I had high hopes of a romance between you two but now you seem to be avoiding each other. What happened?'

Giovanni concentrated on wrapping some mortadella ham around some creamy cheese as he thought about how to answer.

His logical brain had warned him over and over again not to get involved with Annie. It was too soon after the end of his marriage. Ashley had done such a great job of stamping on his heart that he'd thought he'd never love again.

But ... Annie was different from Ashley in every way. She was beautiful, with legs that went on forever and hair that burned gold in the sunlight, but she didn't seem to know it. She certainly didn't use her looks to get what she wanted; he suspected she didn't realise that she could, which was refreshing. She was kind and passionate and determined and every time he met her, he liked her a little more. Until he'd found Annie holding his daughter as they both slept. Then his heart had tipped over the edge and he'd fallen hard.

He wanted to get to know her, and to find out if there could be a future for them. She had shut down his tentative advances straight away. One minute they'd been laughing on the beach and the next she'd been striding away from him. Since then, she'd avoided him completely. He hadn't even bumped into her at his sister's apartment.

It was too dramatic to say that his heart was broken, but it was definitely sore and he didn't know what to do about it. One thing was clear; he may have fallen hard for Annie but she clearly wasn't interested. His logical mind reared its head again and he swore he wasn't going to chase her. He'd get over her soon enough. He hoped.

'Well?' his sister demanded.

'I thought you were against me meeting someone so soon after Ashley,' he prevaricated.

'I never said that. I only said you weren't to get involved with any of the silly women throwing themselves at you. Annie isn't silly. She's lovely, funny, pretty, clever and single. I was sure she was starting to like you. The two of you couldn't keep your eyes off each other, for one thing — but now she avoids coming to see me if she knows you're going to be here. So what have you done?' Giovanni's heart bumped uncomfortably at the thought of Annie unable to keep her eyes off him.

Perhaps there was hope after all.

'Why do you think I've done something?' he asked.

'We grew up together. I've had to comfort countless heartbroken girls over the years.'

He smiled sadly. 'Those days are long over. I do feel bad that I was sometimes a bit cavalier over girlfriends but I'm not like that any more. I honestly don't know what I've done. We were friends one minute, then we weren't. I don't think she likes me in the way you think she does.'

And that really hurt but he would get

over it — he would.

'Hm,' said Carlotta, folding her arms over her chest. 'I don't believe she doesn't like you for a second. There must be something else stopping her. I'll find out what it is and then you can swoop in and do your thing.'

Giovanni concentrated on his plate of food.

'Ah, look at you. You're blushing. How cute!'

Giovanni scowled at his sister. How could someone so helpful be so annoying?

'I'm not cute. I'm —'

A loud knocking at the door interrupted him.

Carlotta glanced at her watch. 'Who can that be at this time?'

'You'll only find out by opening the door,' he teased, glad for the interruption to this uncomfortable conversation.

Carlotta stuck her tongue out at him and he grinned. Whoever it was had taken the heat off him for a moment. It wasn't that he wasn't grateful for his sister's offer of help, but he was old enough to look after his own love life. As she went to let the person in, he snuck some bread off the table and quickly shoved it into his mouth. Hopefully Carlotta wouldn't notice.

Her heard Carlotta's footsteps returning to the kitchen and he chewed faster, the sweet and salty combination making his subterfuge worth it. When he saw Annie trailing behind his sister, he regretted his impulse to stuff his mouth because he suddenly found that he couldn't swallow.

She looked so pale and fragile that he automatically took a step towards her before stopping. If she didn't want his company, she wouldn't welcome a comforting hug, no matter how well—intended. He managed to choke down his mouthful after several unattractive gulps. So much for playing it cool when she was around.

'What's happened?' he croaked.

'I've had a letter,' said Annie, holding up a white A4 envelope. 'It's not good news.'

'Sit down before you fall down,' said Carlotta, pulling out a kitchen chair.

Annie sank onto the proffered seat and Giovanni and Carlotta pulled up chairs next to her. Her slender hands were trembling and Giovanni resisted the urge to take them in his and hold them tightly until she stopped.

She pulled the flap of the envelope open and tugged the papers out.

'I've had to use the internet to translate some of this but I think I've got it right,' she said. 'The general gist seems to be confirmation that Global Hotel has finally submitted formal plans to build a large hotel complex on the land next to the castle. The designs are worse than we initially thought.'

She handed the letter to Giovanni, who quickly skimmed over the letter before standing and spreading the plans out over the work surfaces. Carlotta stood next to him and gasped as she took in the outline.

The complex was almost double the size of the original designs he'd seen, with the new plans showing the monstrosity of a hotel abutting the land he'd newly acquired from Tilly.

He swallowed, but the bread he'd pinched from his sister's table seemed to be stuck in his throat. Carlotta handed him some water and he sipped it, trying to ease the tightness.

'It's worse than we thought, isn't it?' whispered Annie.

'A lot worse!' gasped Carlotta. 'It will destroy the area completely.'

'All is not lost yet, though, is it?' Annie pleaded. 'These are only plans. We can object and they can be stopped, can't they?'

Giovanni shared a look with Carlotta.

'We can try. The thing is, Annie, I don't want to get your hopes up. It's unlikely we'll be successful. The town council are well-known for being easily swayed and for them to have got this far already... I'm sorry.'

'But what about the Roman ruins? Surely there's some sort of preservation order on them. That must count for something.'

'I doubt Global Hotel can build on them, but there's nothing stopping them incorporating them into their hotel. The ruins aren't significant and have never been subject to a preservation order.' Annie sat back in her chair and drummed her fingers on her knees. 'There must be something we can do. I had a neighbour back in Britain who was a lawyer, and she stopped a build happening because of crested newts. Do you have crested newts in Italy?'

'I'm not sure what a crested newt is,' confessed Carlotta.

'I'm not sure either,' said Annie smiling softly. 'I only know that they're endangered and their habitats need to be protected. Perhaps we could import some — although that's probably illegal, isn't it? I don't know.

'I think they're amphibians,' said Giovanni. 'Wouldn't they need to live somewhere wet?'

There was silence as they all remembered how dry and arid the land was.

'There must be something,' insisted

Annie. 'I'll email Liz and ask for her advice, although the last I heard she was in some remote village south of the equator doing conservation work so she might not have time to get back to us. I wish I'd thought of this sooner but it's worth a try.'

'It is,' said Carlotta, patting Annie's arm. 'We'll also organise a protest.'

'And try and raise some money to buy the land ourselves,' added Giovanni, not thinking there was even a small chance that would work but wanting to say something to get rid of the bleakness in Annie's eyes.

'And what about that petition we were thinking about?' asked Annie.

'That too,' said Carlotta, patting Annie's arm again. 'Now, if you'll excuse me I need to sort out Sofia's clothes for the morning. She's off to a theatre camp for the weekend.'

With that, Carlotta whipped out of the kitchen, leaving them alone.

Giovanni knew Carlotta had already prepared everything for Sofia's trip. He hoped Annie didn't realise that too.

He cleared his throat but that didn't help him come up with anything to say. He ran his hands through his hair. He hadn't felt this nervous around a girl since he'd been a gawky teenager. What was wrong with him?

'So ... ' he finally managed.

'I should go,' said Annie, gathering up the documents and shoving them back into the envelope.

'OK,' he said as his heart gave a thud of disappointment. If only he could think of something to say that would make her stay but his mind remained stubbornly blank.

He followed her to the front door, the silence stretching out between them.

'I'm sorry to be the bearer of such awful news,' Annie said as she slipped her shoes on.

He shrugged. 'It's bad, but we knew it was coming. Admittedly we didn't know it was going to be this dire, but still ...'

She turned to face him. 'Do you think there's any chance we'll be able to stop them?'

'I think it's highly unlikely,' he said softly. 'But while there's a small amount of hope we mustn't give up.'

She nodded, her hand resting on the door handle. He expected her to pull it open and to disappear into the night but she stood still looking up at him.

His gaze dropped to her lips. He took a step towards her and brought his hand up to her arm. She didn't move away and so he lightly tugged her towards him, his heart thundering.

Her hand slipped from the door and lightly touched his hip. He sucked in a deep breath. He hadn't realised how much he'd wanted her to touch him until she did. He wanted to pull her against him and kiss her but instinct told him that would be a bad idea.

Slowly, so as not to frighten her off, he gently tucked a strand of hair behind her ear. She turned into his touch and he lightly ran his fingers along her soft jaw.

She sighed quietly and his heart rate kicked up another notch.

Gradually he lowered his head until their lips were touching and then he placed the softest of kisses against her mouth.

He pulled away slightly to judge her reaction but when she didn't run screaming from the room, he kissed her again.

Her arms slid around his waist and pulled him closer. He smiled against her mouth and felt lips curl in response.

For a moment they stayed exactly as they were, kissing in his sister's hallway as if they really were teenagers at the start of a romance.

He was brought back down to earth with the sound of his daughter calling for him and he reluctantly let go of Annie.

'I'd better go,' she said, looking everywhere but at him.

'Annie…' He reached up and caught her arm before she could open the door. 'Don't go yet. I've been thinking about you a lot and I —'

She finally turned to face him and the look on her face was stricken.

'This isn't a good idea,' she said, gesturing between them.

'But if — '

'You're lovely, Giovanni, and I think I could fall for you hard but it would end in tears and I don't want that for either of us. Can we be friends?'

He wanted to argue. A relationship between them didn't have to end badly. He was sure they could make it work. His head was too scrambled to think of the logistics yet, but if they both wanted it enough, then they could find a way.

Before he could get any of his argument out he heard the unmistakable sound of Serena's pounding feet getting closer, so he only nodded. Annie smiled sadly at him and let herself out.

He watched as she ran down the steps towards Carlotta's courtyard and disappeared from view.

She might think things between them would end in tears but he suspected otherwise. He wasn't going to let her go without a fight — especially now they'd kissed. It gave him a small amount of hope and, as he'd just said to Annie, where there was hope then nobody should give up.

19

'I don't think I can manage another piece of cake,' whispered Annie to Giovanni.

'You will have to force it down,' he replied unsympathetically. 'It's considered very bad manners to refuse food.'

'But this will be the fourth piece this afternoon.'

'I told you not to eat lunch.'

'I was hungry then. Now I think I'm going to die.'

'It won't be a bad way to go.' Giovanni fiddled with the cuff of his jumper. 'We want people to sign our petition, which means we have to get them onside. Italian people won't be rushed.'

Annie sank back in the armchair and tried not to think about the million things she still had left to do today. When she'd agreed to help collect signatures for the petition against Global Hotel's proposed development, she'd thought it would be a case of moving from house to house quickly. Either people would want to support them or not. But at almost every residence they'd been invited in and given coffee, or coffee and cake.

Not only was she about to burst from overeating, she was also buzzing from all the caffeine.

Their hostess, a tiny, wrinkled octogenarian who reminded Annie strongly of a raisin, arrived carrying a tray laden with cakes and drinks, putting an end to their whispered conversation.

'Thank you so much for seeing us, Signora Russo,' said Giovanni, taking the tray from her and setting it on a small wooden table.

'It's my pleasure, dear. Please help yourself to a slice of cake. It's a lemon and orange sponge.' Annie was handed a plate and she took a small taste from the corner. It was light and tangy. She took a larger forkful. Giovanni was right; if there was a good way to go, then this was it. Within seconds she'd amazed herself by finishing the whole slice. Where was she putting it?

'I got the fruit from Giovanni,' Signora Russo told Annie. 'He brings me food from his farm now and then. He is a good man, always taking care of people.'

Annie nodded, bemused to notice that the tips of Giovanni's ears had turned a bright scarlet.

'He's handsome too,' Signora Russo added, winking at Annie.

'Oh indeed he is,' agreed Annie, hiding a grin behind a napkin as the redness spread across Giovanni's face. Even though she'd promised herself only to think of him as a friend, she couldn't help noticing how adorable he was when embarrassed.

It took another twenty minutes of small talk before they even got around to talking about Global Hotel. It was excellent Italian practice and Annie realised she was now able to understand all of what was being said despite the older lady's strong accent. Signora Russo seemed particularly fond of Giovanni and she kept extolling his good points, nodding at Annie whenever she did so.

Finally, after what felt like an absolute age, they moved on to Global Hotel and Signora Russo readily agreed to sign their petition.

'I don't know if it will do any good, though. That Lorenzo has always been a greedy boy. He was in school with my son and he always had an extra slice of cake at every party.'

'We can count on your support, can't we?' asked Annie as she popped the petition back into her handbag.

'Of course you can. And I can donate a little money to the fund if you need it. Not much, mind you, but even a little bit could help.'

'We'll be grateful for anything, Signora Russo. Now we'd best leave you to the rest of your afternoon. We've still got quite a few people we need to call on today.'

'Don't bother calling on Nico and his boys. They were saying how much they were looking forward to having a big hotel in the area. Apparently, they are keen to get their hands, and other body

234

parts, on the ladies.'

Annie choked on her last bit of coffee and Giovanni thumped her hard on the back.

'Thank you, we'll give them a miss,' he said, standing up and holding out a hand to Annie to help her up. She took it, giving a little start as his warm skin slid against hers. She tugged her hand away as soon as was polite.

Since those delicious kisses in Carlotta's hallway, she'd had to give herself a firm talking to. Admiring Giovanni and being a friend would have to be enough. Molly came first and she wouldn't live in a different country from her — no matter how handsome the temptation.

After kissing both of Signora Russo's cheeks in a convoluted goodbye, they were finally back on the street. The early March sun was making an appearance after a week of rain and Annie tilted her face to the warmth.

'I think you have an admirer,' Annie teased as they moved down the street.

Giovanni laughed but the tips of his

ears turned pink again.

'It was very sweet,' she said.

She didn't want to embarrass him but she found it curiously endearing the way he kept blushing. Surely he was used to people admiring his looks by now. He had been a model after all.

'I think it was all for your benefit,' he mumbled.

'What do you mean?'

'I think she was pointing out what a good catch I am. In case you hadn't noticed for yourself.' He shot her a quick grin before knocking the door of Signora Russo's neighbour.

It was her turn to burn red as a wave of embarrassment swept over her.

Thankfully Giovanni was soon occupied in talking to a young woman who seemed more than happy to flick her hair and smile at Giovanni while he spoke. Annie fanned her face, hoping she would return to her normal temperature by the time he'd finished talking.

Luckily they weren't invited in for yet more food and Giovanni was able to get

236

the woman's signature within a matter of minutes.

'That went well,' she said inanely as they ventured further down the street.

'Yes, she was very anti-Global Hotel and was happy to sign.'

She was probably swayed more with Giovanni's looks than any passionate desire to stop the building, thought Annie and then she shook her head. She had turned Giovanni down, and so she had no right to be jealous when another woman noticed how attractive he was.

As Giovanni knocked on the next door, she couldn't help wondering whether she had been a monumental fool the other night. Walking away from him had been one of the hardest things she'd ever done. Her mind knew she had made the right decision, but her heart was protesting very loudly that she was making a dreadful mistake.

She would ring Molly later. Talking to her daughter always served to remind her of what was most important in life.

'How's Tilly getting on with purchasing

that other hotel?' asked Giovanni, when he failed to get a response to his knock.

'She's finally worn them down and they've accepted her offer but she still has to stay on the other side of the island to complete paperwork.'

'So you're still not getting any help with the decorating?'

'No — but to be honest, where Tilly's concerned, it's not such a bad thing. She's absolutely dreadful with a paint-brush. I'm aiming for a smooth-wall finish and if I let Tilly loose for more than a few minutes she covers surfaces in blobs, which I then have to sand down and go over in secret so as not to hurt her feelings.'

Giovanni laughed and Annie smiled in delight at having amused him. The smile soon faded as they plodded on with only a smattering of success.

'Can we call it a day soon?' asked Annie after ten more houses. 'I'm get-ting tired.'

Giovanni glanced at his watch. 'Is that the time? I said I'd get Serena from my parents an hour ago. Come on!'

As Giovanni had driven her to this area which she didn't know well, she had no choice but to follow him as he raced back to his car.

She didn't want to become more embroiled in his family. It was bad enough that Carlotta had become such a good friend, and that Serena was one of the most adorable little girls she'd ever met, without adding his parents into the mix.

'You can drop me near the centre of town, if you like,' she said as she fastened her seatbelt. 'I can walk back to the castle from there.'

'I won't make you walk after all that traipsing around today,' he said, flashing her a smile as he pulled out into the road. 'It won't take long at my parents, and then I'll drop you home.'

There was nothing for it; she would have to meet his parents after all. She just had to hope they were horrible and terribly off-putting and that they would make her feel dreadfully uncomfortable around their son. She would have another reason to harden her heart against him then.

Giovanni's parents lived a short drive from the outskirts of Vescovina. Their long driveway was lined with fruit trees and the sun was setting over the pale pink house as Giovanni brought the car to a stop.

'Shall I wait in the car?' Annie asked hopefully. Giovanni snorted in amusement.

'Haven't you learned anything about Vescovinian hospitality? You have to come in and have a drink at the very least. I'm pretty sure they'll try to feed you too. Also, Serena will want to know what calamities have befallen you today.'

'Calamities?'

'You know, whether you've hit someone or become stuck up a cliff face. That sort of thing.'

Annie laughed despite herself.

She didn't want to step into this beautiful home. She feared her heart might be totally lost if his parents turned out to be even half as lovely as their children.

She hadn't had much of a home-life growing up. Her parents loved her, but they also loved their careers and often the job won out. She stayed in boarding school during term-time and travelled to wherever they were during the holidays. If that hadn't been possible — Australia was too far to go for a week — she'd stayed with Tilly.

Tilly was fantastic fun and she'd loved spending time with her but that hadn't stopped Annie fantasising over a traditional family. She'd imagined a home with a loving mother who'd always welcome her with loving arms and a big, squashy, comfortable dad. She'd hoped to have that for herself one day with a house full of children, but she'd only had five years of married life before that too was whisked away from her.

She gave herself a little shake. She was being overdramatic. This was only one drink, and then they could be on their way.

A small dog shot out from around the

back of the house, barking madly, tail a blur of action. He launched himself at Giovanni, who laughed and scooped the dog up.

'Hey, Bandit, you always give the best welcomes. No one else is ever this pleased to see me. I hope you like dogs,' he said to Annie. 'This one will love you regardless of who you are.'

'I love dogs,' said Annie. 'I've always wanted one of my own but I had to work and it didn't seem fair leaving a dog in the house all day.'

'Come and say hello, then, but be prepared to be licked to death.'

Sure enough, Bandit covered her proffered hand in enthusiastic licks.

'That's enough, Bandit. Have some pride. Women don't like it if you're too obvious,' said Giovanni, moving the dog away from her. 'Sorry, I did warn you. Right let's go and see everyone. I should warn you, my mother loves to talk and will want to know everything about you. You can tell her to mind her own business if you want to, everyone does.'

He placed Bandit on the floor before leading the way to the back of the house. Bandit leapt between them with increasing enthusiasm.

Serena was equally enthusiastic to see her father and threw herself at him in delight. Reluctant to step into the welcoming family circle Annie hung back until a man who could only be Giovanni's father stepped forward and surprised her by pulling her into a big hug.

'You must be Annie,' he boomed. 'We've heard so much about you.'

'Oh,' said Annie, who was released only to be swept up by Giovanni's mother.

'Carlotta nearly dies with laughter every time she tells the story of you hitting Giovanni with a shopping basket,' she said, releasing Annie only a little so that she could get a good look at her. 'You do have the most beautiful eyes,' she said. 'They're very unusual.'

Annie, who had always considered her grey eyes rather dull, was surprised at this statement. Giovanni and Carlotta had remarkable eyes particularly considering their dark skin, but hers were nothing out of the ordinary.

'Giovanni tells me you're a widow,' said Giovanni's mother, tugging Annie over to a bench. 'How awful for you when you are still so young. And he also said you're a mother. Come and tell me all about yourself.'

A glass of wine was thrust into Annie's hand and she took a long sip of the deliciously rich liquid before his mother carried on.

'I'm Viola and my husband is Grigor. I can't believe my son hasn't introduced us.'

'You didn't give me a chance, Mama,' laughed Giovanni. 'I'm sorry, Annie. I did warn you about my mother but I guess she is even worse in person. She is considered to be one of the nosiest people on the island.'

Viola sucked in a shocked breath.

'Do you see what I have put up with, Annie? My son tells terrible mistruths. I'm not nosy, I'm inquisitive. Now, tell me, how did your day go?'

'There was a lot of cake,' said Annie, slightly bewildered by this whirlwind of a woman.

Viola nodded. 'We like our food here in Vescovina. Oh yes, Giovanni, go and tell your father to set an extra place at the dinner table.'

Annie wasn't sure if that place was for her or not but she didn't think she'd get away with leaving even if she wanted to.

'We got a handful of signatures,' said Annie. 'I don't think it's enough but hopefully the others did better.'

'Yes, I heard from Carlotta earlier and she was quite pleased with how her day had gone.'

When Annie arrived at Carlotta's apartment earlier in the day she'd expected to be partnered with Carlotta. She was sure Greta wouldn't want to miss the opportunity of an afternoon of flirting with Giovanni, but she'd been surprised. Carlotta and Greta were already discussing the route they would take around town and it hadn't been suggested that she go with them. They'd left suspiciously fast and if Annie didn't know better, she'd have thought Carlotta was matchmaking. But Carlotta thought women who made a fool of themselves over Giovanni were silly and so she must have been mistaken.

'Hopefully together the petitions will make a difference,' said Annie, trying to focus on the most important point of the day.

'I'm sure they will, my dear. Now, come through to the kitchen, we're about to eat.'

A plate of gigantic ravioli in creamy sauce was placed in front of her. Even though she was full of cake, Annie found she had room for it.

'I had some good news while you two were sitting chatting outside,' said Giovanni when they'd all finished scraping their bowls. 'Greta's husband has offered to donate a sizeable sum to our fund.'

'That is good news,' said Annie, pleased for her friend. Greta had feared Piero would want to invest in Global

Hotel's development, rather than the land it was threatening to destroy. She must have persuaded him that it would be bad for Vescovina. If she could persuade her husband, then hopefully they'd have success in bringing other residents round to their cause.

'It's the protest on Saturday, isn't it?' Viola asked her son.

'Yes — will you be there?'

'Of course we'll be there. I'm looking forward to it. I haven't been to a good protest since I was a teenager. I'll be waving those banners and swearing like a trooper, don't you worry.'

Annie giggled at the look on Giovanni's face. 'Mama, I'm not sure it's going to be that dramatic.'

'Don't worry, son. I'll make sure it is.' She winked at Annie as Giovanni rolled his eyes.

'I think that's our sign to call it a night,' said Giovanni, standing and stretching.

Annie found it very difficult to tear her eyes from the sliver of taut stomach muscles he revealed as he did so. It was unfair just how attractive he really was. She was already half in love with his family. He didn't need to flaunt his body as well.

Annie was hugged and kissed by both his parents and she longed to stay in the warmness and happiness of their beautiful home. She tore herself away and climbed into the car, fastening her seatbelt and promising herself that she wasn't falling in love with Giovanni's family.

By the time Giovanni had strapped Serena into her car seat and clambered into the car himself she was on the verge of tears, which was ridiculous. She wished, more than anything, that she could transport this wonderful family to Britain, where she could be with them and her precious daughter. But it was impossible.

Soon her work at the castle would be over and she would return home. Her time with Giovanni's family and working in this magical part of the world would be over. And all she'd worked for would be ruined by a huge corporation that didn't care what they did to the environment and whose lives they ruined, so long as they made a profit.

Her breath caught and she turned her head to look out of the window at the starry evening.

'Are you all right?' Giovanni asked softly as he drove slowly down the narrow driveway.

'Mmm,' she murmured, not wanting him to know that tears were now leaking down her face. He seemed to sense it anyway because he only drove a short way down the country lane before pulling over and stopping the car.

'Are you crying?'

'Sorry, Giovanni. I'm so very tired. I'm working so hard and it's going to be for nothing, isn't it?'

'No, we won't let Global Hotel win. We will fight this. I'll lie in front of their bulldozers if I have to.'

Annie giggled through her tears. 'I'd like to see that.'

'Yeah, I'm sure you would.' He laughed gently.

'Please don't cry.'

His soft voice only served to make the tears come faster. He unclipped her seatbelt and pulled her into a tight hug. After a few minutes of crying into his jumper she felt two little arms curl around her neck and the light weight of a small child curling into her back.

Who was she kidding? She wasn't half in love with this man and his family. She was completely and irrevocably in love with all of them and she was beginning to suspect they loved her too.

She'd have to tread carefully for the next few months to make sure it was only her heart that was broken when she moved back to Britain.

20

Bookings now available at this bespoke, boutique hotel. Email for availability and rates. Annie leaned back in her chair. Was bespoke and boutique too much? She deleted bespoke, and decided boutique wasn't quite enough.

She'd always believed a job in marketing was an easy option, all you had to do was add superlative words to glossy pictures. But it was much harder than it looked. She was rubbish at it.

All she wanted to do was add a post to Twitter, advertising the opening of the hotel. An hour in, and all words had been deleted only to add them back minutes later and then delete it again.

She looked at the photograph she'd taken of the castello from a distance. It looked stunning against a brilliant blue sky and rolling countryside. Perhaps the photograph would speak for itself. She cleared the screen and tried again.

Email now and book your room at this unique hotel on the stunning Isola di Cigni. Early booking discounts are available.

She clicked on the post button before she could change the sentence again. She was beginning to annoy herself with her own indecisiveness. She turned her computer off, stood and stretched.

'Did you get it done?' asked Greta, coming up behind her.

'I went for the easy option and told it like it is. It turns out I'm not great at marketing campaigns.'

'Hm, well at least it's done now and you can stop boring everybody about it.'

'Hey,' laughed Annie. 'You're very rude.'

Greta put her hand on her hip and pouted. 'So what if I am. Are you going to fire me?'

'Not on your life. You're not going anywhere.'

Greta had been a godsend over the last few weeks. When she'd realised Annie was in desperate need of help at the castle she'd volunteered to be a general dogsbody. Annie had explained there was no money to pay her, but Greta didn't mind. With only a few weeks until the hotel opened, Annie needed all the help she could get.

'Perhaps the next shot should be of me enjoying the rooftop pool. I could be drinking some prosecco in the early evening sun. Oooh, better yet, get a picture of Giovanni in there as the local farmer. You'll have a flood of bookings. Oooh, even better yet! Have Giovanni and me in the roof top pool sipping prosecco but make sure he knows he's not to wear many clothes.'

Annie gave a snort of laughter. 'It's not a bad idea to get a couple of photos but I think, lovely though you undoubtedly are, I don't need anyone in them. The hotel is gorgeous enough as it is. I'm certainly not going to ask Giovanni.'

'You're certainly not going to ask me what?' asked a deep voice. Annie's heart sank as she turned to find Giovanni frowning at her from the entrance to the hotel.

'I was saying to Annie that you can help advertise the hotel by stripping off and posing in the rooftop pool.' Greta jumped in before Annie could say anything.

'I'm not sure how that would attract customers,' said Giovanni, his frown still in place but a hint of amusement lurking in his sea-blue eyes.

'We'd take pictures, of course, and post them on social media implying you're here all the time. We'd be inundated with bookings.'

Annie was so embarrassed by Greta's comments she didn't know where to look. She certainly couldn't even glance at Giovanni.

'It's great to know you think I'm good for something, Greta,' Giovanni commented dryly. 'Annie, I was coming to see you and met the postman on my way. These are for you.'

Unable to look him in the eye Annie took the proffered letters and began to flick through them as Greta and Giovanni bickered politely in the background. It was mostly bills, which Annie piled on the newly installed reception desk. Tilly could see to those. There was also one cheque for a week's booking in July, and she made sure to put this on top to soften the blow of the rest.

The last letter made her knees go weak and she leaned against the counter to support herself.

Greta was explaining to Giovanni how Annie could arrange him artfully on the terrace but Annie was too shocked by the envelope's contents to be embarrassed any more.

It took a few moments for her distress to filter through to the others.

'Annie, what's wrong?' asked Giovanni, stepping towards her.

'It's a letter from the council,' said Annie quietly. 'They are writing to let us know that Global Hotel has been given permission to build on the land adjacent to the castle. Construction will begin in September.'

Silence greeted her announcement.

'All the letter writing, protesting and

petition — gathering were a waste of time.' Annie's voice cracked. 'Everyone's going to be so disappointed.' She shoved the letter back into the envelope.

'Oh, Annie,' whispered Greta.

'It's not over until the first brick is put down,' said Giovanni stoutly.

Annie shook her head. 'I don't know how you can be positive. This is a disaster.'

'I'll make a cup of tea,' said Greta. 'That's how you deal with a crisis in Britain, isn't it?'

Before Annie could stop her, Greta had disappeared in the direction of the castle's kitchen. She wished people would stop throwing her and Giovanni together.

He came and leaned against the reception desk next to her, his arm touching hers. She longed to lean into him but knew it would be wrong. She shouldn't give the impression that he meant anything more to her than any of her other Italian friends.

'What was it you wanted to talk to me

about?' she asked after a few minutes of silence.

'I ... do you know what, it can wait.' He glanced at his watch. 'In fact I'd better be heading off. I need to pick up Serena. I'll see you soon, Annie.'

'OK,' she said quietly as he moved away from her towards the entrance.

Greta returned with a tray of tea just as the door closed behind him.

'Where's he gone?' she asked, her eyes round with surprise.

'He had to pick up Serena.'

Greta glanced at the time. 'But it's only...' She caught sight of Annie's face and stopped.

'It's all a bit of a mess,' said Annie, taking her mug of tea and sipping it gratefully.

'It can be sorted out.'

'How?'

'Well, I would imagine it's fairly easy. Pop round there later today and tell him you're sorry and you made a mistake. I'm sure he'll understand.'

'What are you talking about?'

' Giovanni. Why? What were you talking about?'

'I was talking about Global Hotel! What on earth made you think I was talking about Giovanni?'

'Well, um... he left and I thought you two had fallen out.'

Annie threw her hands up into the air. 'Even if I had fallen out with Giovanni, I don't see why it would matter — and what do you mean by 'I've made a mistake'?'

Greta shuffled her feet. Annie was hit by a pang of guilt for making her friend uncomfortable but she wanted to get to the bottom of Greta's comments so she didn't apologise.

'I know I shouldn't have said anything,' said Greta guiltily. 'But we can all see that you and Giovanni are perfect for each other and no one can understand why you aren't together.'

'Who's *we all*?'

'Everybody.'

Annie brushed some fluff off the desk. 'I know Giovanni is lovely but the

258

thing is, I can't live in Italy so there's no point in a relationship with him. I'm not going to live so far away from Molly and that's the end of it.'

'Molly would want you to be happy,' Greta said softly.

'I know she would, but I won't be happy if I'm too far away from her — so please can we drop the subject and concentrate on the disaster that is Global Hotel and their monstrosity of a building.'

Greta nodded slowly.

'Of course we can, although right now I can't think of anything to say about it so I think it's best if I carry on with painting the bathroom upstairs. Give me a shout if you want to mull over any ideas.'

And with that, Greta left Annie alone. She tried to convince herself that was exactly what she wanted but she couldn't shake off the feeling that everything was falling apart.

21

Annie opened the parcel at her feet and crowed in delight. Her box of specially designed paperwork had arrived. She could spend a happy morning not worrying about anything other than where to put it all.

She lifted out the first bound packet and discovered printed postcards. She inhaled the fresh glue smell and sighed happily. She'd put a postcard in every room. The guests would be welcome to take them away, or they could use them to send to friends or relatives. Either way it was good promotion — and so pretty.

From somewhere nearby, her mobile rang. She scrabbled around in the packaging.

'Molly,' she called when she finally located it and hit answer. 'How lovely to hear from you. How are things?'

'Everything's good, Mum. I'm trying to revise at the moment, although the weather's gorgeous and so I'm finding it hard to do anything other than sunbathe. Anyway, that's not why I'm ringing. Do you remember our old neighbour, Liz? The lawyer.'

Annie's heart quickened. 'Yes, I remember her. Why?'

'She rang me yesterday. She was trying to get hold of you but she'd forgotten your number and deleted the email you sent her. For some reason she had mine. Anyway, I gave yours to her again so hopefully she'll be in touch. Why would you email her after all this time?'

'I contacted her because I want her advice about something legal to do with Aunt Tilly's hotel. Did she say when she'd get in touch?'

'No. You remember what she was like, though, don't you? She was as sharp as a whip in court but quite scatterbrained about everything else.'

'Did you get her number?' said Annie, crossing her fingers tightly. This might be the break they so desperately needed.

'I did — hang on.'

Molly reeled off the numbers, which Annie scribbled on one of her new post-cards.

'Thanks, Molly, that's great. Now, about your revising...'

They chattered for a while, Annie content to hear her daughter speak even though the thought of Molly not working very hard made her feel a bit wobbly. They'd pooled all their resources into getting Molly to university; she didn't want her daughter to throw this opportunity away.

'Mum,' said Molly, as their phone call wound to an end. 'I'm kidding ab out the revising. I don't want you to take that comment seriously. I promise you, I'm working around the clock. I'm going to make you proud.'

Annie's heart clenched.

'You make me proud all the time, Molly.'

'Thanks, Mum.'

'That doesn't mean you should stop, though ...' Annie heard Molly's laughter as she ended the call. She smiled indulgently at the handset for a moment and then gave herself a little shake. It was time to call Liz.

Annie's fingers trembled as she typed in the number. So much was riding on this call.

'Hello,' came her former neighbour's brusque voice as she answered the phone.

'Oh, hello Liz, this is Annie. I hope you don't mind but Molly passed on your number.'

'Oh, yes, hello Annie. I've been thinking about your email. You've got yourself an interesting problem. I've been giving it a lot of thought.'

'You have?' said Annie, pleased that she didn't have to bother with small talk before getting straight to the point.

'Yes. It's a nasty company you're up against. They've been taken to court several times over their builds but no one's ever been successful.'

'Oh,' said Annie, her heart plummeting.

'But if you dig a little deeper some interesting facts come up.'

'Really? Is the owner a criminal or

something?'

Liz let out a bark of laughter, 'No. You won't find any dirt on the company. Ruthless they may be, but they never leave themselves open to being sued. You'll need to be smarter than that.'

'What do you mean?'

'Occasionally, very occasionally I should stress, they are stopped before they can start.'

'But how?'

'It's not so much Global Hotel you want to stop, but the people or company that are allowing them to develop the land they want. I've read of two cases where this strategy has worked successfully. It's only moved the situation elsewhere, mind you, but that's a problem for another day.'

Annie sagged into a chair.

'We've tried that. The town planner appears to be the person who's letting them get away with it. We've petitioned him, protested outside his work, I've even confronted him. Nothing works. The man has the skin of a rhino and the heart of... well, a thing without a heart.'

'He's probably accepting some back-handers.'

'That's the rumour. We've no way of proving it.'

'Then you have to find something that means more to him than backhanders. Look, I've got to go. Let me know how you get on.'

And with that Liz was gone, with Annie no wiser as to how to proceed. She went back to her box of stationery but her earlier enthusiasm had disappeared. She dumped everything back into the box and stood up. She'd walk down to Giovanni's and let him know their final hope had led to nothing.

As she walked over the uneven terrain that separated the castle from Giovanni's land, she tried to convince herself that going to him was purely a business courtesy and nothing more. By the time she'd reached his front door, she'd almost done it.

It wasn't until he pulled the door open wearing a faded-blue T-shirt and pale jeans that a tiny bit of her admitted that she'd come to see him to make her feel better. His welcoming smile made her stomach somersault and she couldn't help but beam back at him.

'Hey,' he said. 'Come on in.'

He held the door wide for her and the unmistakable smell of burning food hit her as she stepped over the threshold. She pulled a face and Giovanni laughed.

'Please ignore the smell. Serena and I have been baking cakes but apparently I'm not as good at it as Auntie Carlotta.'

'Did you cook them for too long?'

'You could say that,' Giovanni grinned. 'Come through to the kitchen. We're having a second attempt so please ignore the mess and try and find a spot that isn't sticky.'

Annie laughed as she followed Giovanni. He wasn't wrong about the mess. Sticky dough seemed to cover the entire kitchen table and quite a bit of the floor. Serena was enthusiastically licking a spoon, which she waved at Annie as she entered the room, spraying blobs of white matter around, some of which landed in her hair.

Giovanni groaned.

'Now she'll have to have a bath.'

Annie took in the small child covered almost head-to-toe in batter.

'I'm fairly sure she needed one anyway.'

'True but her hair is a nightmare to wash and I was really hoping to avoid having to do it. Anyway I'm sure you didn't come here to talk about baths. Why don't you take a seat while Serena and I put this mixture into the cupcake cases and then you can tell me what it is you came to say?'

Annie pulled out the nearest chair and, finding it clean, sank down onto it. Giovanni helped Serena ladle teaspoons of batter into pink polka-dotted cases. Serena was using the same spoon she'd been licking so enthusiastically. Annie grinned — the delights of parenthood.

Her smile faded as she remembered the reason for her visit.

'I had a chat with my lawyer friend and I'm afraid it wasn't helpful.'

'What did she have to say?'

Annie related their conversation, 'So you see, it's not really been any help,' she finished.

Giovanni helped Serena down from her chair and led her over to the sink, 'You're thinking of it in terms of protesting, but I think your friend meant something different.'

He wiped Serena's hands with a cloth and then dabbed at her dress. 'I think that will do for now. Why don't you go and play while I put the cakes in the oven and chat to Annie.'

'Remember not to burn them this time, Papà.'

'Of course I won't make the same mistake again.'

Serena giggled, 'Silly Papà.'

She gave Annie a sticky kiss on her way past and Annie's heart squeezed. She was lovely.

'How long do you think they should take?' Giovanni asked as he slid the tray into the oven.

'You've got the oven too high, for a

start,' she said, bustling over to take a look. 'Turn it right down. Then I'd check them after fifteen minutes.'

Giovanni fiddled with the dial.

'I think your lawyer has made a good point. Perhaps we have been going about this the wrong way. Instead of trying to appeal to Lorenzo Moretti's good side, as he obviously doesn't have one, we should be looking at what he wants.'

Annie took a step backwards.

'You think we should try to bribe him?'

Giovanni grinned his heart-stopping smile. 'Look at your face. You'd think I'd just suggested we have him killed. No, I don't think we should bribe him. We probably couldn't compete with the bribes Global Hotel is giving him anyway. No, I was thinking of something subtler than that. What does Lorenzo Moretti want most of all?'

Giovanni waggled his eyebrows and Annie couldn't help giggling.

'I have no idea.'

'He wants to be re-elected.'

'And we can stop that how?'

'Ah,' said Giovanni, leaning his hip against the work surface. 'I haven't thought of that yet.'

'We can't exactly threaten him with the people who signed our petition voting against him. Even if we could persuade them to all vote the same, and the canvassing alone would be insane, there probably aren't enough people on that list to make a difference.'

'Hm. OK, I need to give it some more thought.' He began to run the hot water and to dump dishes into the sink. Annie picked up a tea towel and waited by the dish drainer.

'Oh no, you don't have to do that. You're a guest. Sit down, I'll get you a drink or something.'

'I'll have a cake when they're ready.'

'I don't think that's a good idea, I don't want to poison you. I've probably got some of Carlotta's in the cupboard somewhere.'

'I wouldn't want to offend Serena by eating someone else's cake. Besides, as much as I like sitting down and eating, I come up with better ideas if I'm moving around.'

Giovanni pushed a damp hand through his hair, making it stand up on end. 'OK, I won't protest too much. It'll take me hours on my own.'

For a while they washed and dried in comfortable silence. Annie slipped into a daydream where this was her life on a daily basis, then shook her head. Nothing could come of thoughts like that.

'I'll go get my laptop,' said Giovanni as Annie wiped over a large mixing bowl. 'Maybe we'll find some inspiration if we can discover anything about Global Hotel's stalled developments.'

Giovanni left the kitchen seconds before the oven timer pinged. Slipping on oven gloves, Annie pulled out the tray of cakes. The tops were golden brown and when she touched them gently, the sponge sprang back. Serena would be pleased that this time, they seemed to have got it right. She lifted the little cakes out of the baking tray and onto a rack to cool.

'Hey, these actually look good,' said Giovanni as he carried his computer over to the kitchen table. 'We should try one before Serena covers them in brightly coloured icing and sprinkles.'

'I'm not averse to a sprinkle but I will try a freshly baked one now.'

Together they munched on the small sponges, which were crunchy on the outside but soft in the middle, as Giovanni scrolled through pages of irrelevant websites.

Annie's eyes glazed over after a few minutes of trying to translate the unwieldy text into English. Giovanni ploughed on until he finally seemed to hit on something. He sat upright in his chair.

'Look at this. This is really interesting.' Annie squinted at the screen.

'I can't make head or tail of it. My reading of Italian is not that good. What does it say?'

Giovanni went on scrolling through the wording. 'Yes,' he said. 'This is fantastic. I think we might have got him.'

22

Annie gripped the moped's handlebars tightly as she made her way through the winding streets of Vescovina and out towards its port. A small bump in the road set her heart pounding but she kept going. She'd never make it if she stopped the bike and walked.

She was going to be late as it was, but she didn't want to miss it altogether. Not that she'd be a great deal of help... but she needed to be there to support Giovanni.

Finally she pulled into a narrow parking space and climbed gratefully off the vehicle. She only really used the moped for the journey between the castle and the cottage, and that was only when she knew she'd be staying late decorating. Otherwise she walked everywhere, because getting on the bike was still terrifying — even if she did go at the speed of a snail.

She cut through the car park and arrived at the front of the headquarters of the local fishing community. It was a large, white building, where a loose union of fishermen worked to protect their own interests and who might be the very people who could stop Global Hotel in their tracks. Because the hotel was being built on land, they'd not thought to approach the union before — but their recent research had changed all that.

Taking a deep breath, she stepped inside the cool atrium and made her way over to the reception desk.

'Buon pomeriggio,' she said to the austere-looking receptionist. 'I'm here for the meeting.'

'They've already started.'

'Yes, I know I'm a little late but I'd like to slip in the back to see how it's going. I'll be quiet.'

The woman gave a brisk nod. 'OK, follow the corridor until the double-doors and then take a left. It's the first room on the right.'

Annie hurried down the corridor,

crossing her fingers that everything was going well. Giovanni was presenting his findings to the large fishing community. All he had planned to say represented hours of not only their work and research into Global Hotel's impact on aquatic life, but that of their friends and family too. There was so much riding on the next hour and Giovanni's performance.

She slipped into the room and caught sight of Viola, leaning against the back wall and watching her son speak. Annie sidled up to her and whispered, 'How's it going so far?'

'They're all listening attentively so I'd say it's going well.'

Annie flashed her a thumbs up and turned to face the front of the room where Giovanni was standing behind a lectern exuding confidence and authority.

He nodded to a gentleman in the front row who had his hand up. 'Yes, sir?'

'How do we know you're telling us the truth?'

'I have sourced information and double and triple checked it. You are welcome to read my notes and all the accompanying evidence after this meeting. I have nothing to hide — unlike Global Hotel.

'I understand that more tourists in the area means more mouths to feed, which in theory should raise your profits, but the reality isn't the case. Global Hotel import all their food and never use local produce. The evidence is clear, however, that where Global Hotel builds their large complexes the marine life is badly affected — not only with increased traffic in the seas but the increased sewage. If we allow this build to go ahead, there will be a huge impact on your livelihoods.'

The men shifted in their seats and low-level muttering broke out through the crowd. Giovanni let it continue for a moment before stopping them by knocking his fist against the lectern.

'What can we do?' asked the same man who'd called out before. 'You said you've tried protesting. So why do you think we can help put a stop to Global

Hotel's plans?'

'Our community depends on the fishing industry. There's not a family who won't be affected if the marine life disappears, and it will have a devastating impact on our town's way of life. If you, as a working body, can put political pressure on Lorenzo Moretti, then I think we stand a good chance of him rescinding the approval.'

Louder muttering. Giovanni raised a hand. 'I've said what I've come to say. If any of you want to talk about this further please come and talk about the evidence with me — or with my colleague, Annie, at the back there.'

Annie's heart jolted as the audience swivelled to look in her direction. She just had to hope her Italian didn't let her down if anyone did come to talk to her. Although she was now mostly fluent, some technical terms still threw her.

Talking broke out as Giovanni began to pack away his slides and extensive notes. For a moment Annie thought it was going to be like their talk in Carlotta's cafe all those months ago when most of the attendees left at the end of the talk. She was wrong.

For another hour, both she and Giovanni talked and talked. They discussed the evidence they'd unearthed over the last week showing how depleted fish stocks often occurred around Global Hotel's developments and how several small fishing communities had been destroyed. Annie began to hope that all their work hadn't been in vain. Finally the leader shook Giovanni's hand and thanked them both for coming.

'We'll get back to you to let you know what we decide to do. It will be put to the vote as to whether we act or not.'

'Thank you for taking the time to listen to what we had to say,' said Giovanni.

The other man smiled. 'Thank you for taking the time to come and tell us. I, for one, am convinced you speak the truth and maybe you have saved us all from an absolute disaster.'

Giovanni smiled back and Annie's heart stuttered; this could be the turning point.

'Well done, mio figlio,' said Viola as the last of the attendees melted away. 'You gave a very impressive speech and both of you really knew your stuff afterwards. Whatever happens now, you know that you've tried your absolute best.'

'So long as our absolute best produces the results we want, then I'm happy,' said Giovanni. 'Well there's nothing else you can do today.

Your dad and I will take care of Serena for a while longer. Why don't you take Annie out for dinner?'

Viola kissed them both goodbye and left before they could protest.

'I'm sorry about my mother,' said Giovanni when Viola had skipped away to her car. 'She means well but no matter how many times I tell her you're not interested in me, she doesn't believe it. I guess that's mothers for you.'

Heat rushed over Annie's face at his words. They'd worked so hard this last week, gathering evidence and writing Giovanni's speech that any romantic feelings had been pushed to one side. There had been a few occasions when his sister or Greta had deliberately left them alone together. Annie had cringed but she'd got through it by thinking he'd not noticed.

'Er...' she started.

'I'm sorry, I didn't mean to embarrass you. I thought it might be easier to tell it like it is rather than pretend not to notice everyone pushing us together all the time. From the look on your face I may have made the wrong call.'

Annie braved looking up at him. He was smiling a slightly lopsided grin but his eyes were sad.

'Let's go to dinner,' she said. 'My treat.'

Giovanni looked at her for a long moment. 'OK, there's a good pizzeria around the corner. We can get a takeaway, sit on the harbour wall.'

'Sounds lovely,' she said, setting off. 'What topping do you recommend?'

They talked about Serena and Molly as they ordered their food, then carried the warm slices over to the harbour wall. Giovanni wanted to know what pitfalls of parenting were coming up as Serena entered her teenage years and had Annie laughing as he gave his opinion on boy-friends.

'None, not ever. I know what goes through young men's minds and it's not pretty.'

The harbour was full of fishing vessels and expensive-looking yachts.

'Growing up, I always thought I'd own one of those,' said Annie, pointing to a particularly impressive yacht. 'But it turns out I couldn't even afford one of those.' She indicated a dinghy.

Giovanni laughed. 'I get badly seasick, so even if I could afford one I wouldn't want it anyway.'

'Do you? How sick do you get?'

'I'm completely unable to move apart from when I need to throw up. I took Serena on a pedalo once thinking I'd be OK. It wasn't.'

Annie giggled.

'Thank you for your words of comfort,' said Giovanni dryly.

'Sorry but you don't look like a man who would let a wave beat you.'

'It doesn't need to be wavy. The water can be as still as a millpond and I will still be unwell.'

Annie laughed out loud, 'Hugo was going to take me on a cruise for our tenth wedding anniversary, which would have been around my thirtieth birthday. We were so young when we married, we had absolutely no money. We camped in a muddy field for our honeymoon and so we made it our goal to cruise on the Mediterranean in luxury.'

'That sounds like a good thing to aim for,' said Giovanni softly.

'It was,' said Annie, smiling as she remembered the two of them, so young and in love and absolutely not bothered about all their belongings being covered in thick, black mud. 'Obviously it didn't happen. I had barely enough money to send Molly to school in new clothes by the time I was thirty and now everything I earn has to go on paying for university. I can't imagine I'll ever get to go on a luxury liner. But it doesn't matter — looking after Molly was worth sacrificing an expensive holiday for.'

'Has it always been you two since Hugo died?'

Annie nodded, watching a bright-blue fishing boat chug back towards the harbour.

'Have you never been tempted to get together with someone else?'

His eyes, a brilliant blue in the bright sunshine, were watching her face intently. She reached over and took his hand in hers. His skin was warm and dry and his fingers curled around hers.

'I've never been tempted until recently,' she said sadly. 'It's not that I don't want to be with you, Giovanni. I want to be part of your life so badly it hurts. But Molly comes first. I'm sorry.'

Giovanni nodded, his gaze now fixed on where their hands were joined. 'I know.' He laughed softly. 'That you put your daughter first is one of the many reasons I love you so much.'

23

Annie wound the last of the fairy lights around a potted tree that stood on the edge of the terrace and stepped back to admire her handiwork.

Guests would soon start arriving for a party to celebrate the completion of the hotel. Carlotta was busy in the kitchen preparing the food and Tilly was spinning around the place tweaking cushions and smoothing out tablecloths.

Their first paying guests would be arriving next week but tonight was all about celebrating the work Annie, and everyone else involved, had put in to create this beautiful hotel.

'There you are.' Tilly emerged from the dining room in a long, white, floaty dress. 'I wanted to talk to you before everyone else arrives.'

'Is everything all right?' asked Annie anxiously. They were still waiting to hear from the council as to whether or not the Global Hotel build was going ahead. Now that the fishing industry had said they wouldn't support their local politicians if it did, everyone was confident that Global Hotel's scheme would collapse. But Annie wasn't going to celebrate until they had official confirmation.

'Everything is perfect,' said Tilly, slipping her arm around Annie and giving her a reassuring squeeze. 'You are an absolute star and a complete genius. The hotel couldn't look more spectacular, but then I knew you would do a fabulous job and I am never wrong.'

Annie laughed. 'What about that time with the firewood?'

'We agreed never to talk about that again.'

'I know but I can't help thinking of it when you make such outrageous claims. I don't think your neighbour was ever the same after that incident.'

Tilly snorted. 'OK, there was the time with the firewood and another time with a cactus plant which I also never talk about, but apart from those two times

I'm never wrong. I certainly wasn't wrong about you. You've really blossomed over the last eight months and I'm so proud of you.'

Annie's heart swelled with love. 'Thank you.'

'It's why I've got an offer for you.' Tilly paused. 'I still haven't found anyone to manage the hotel.'

'I don't think you're looking hard enough. That woman we saw last week was eminently capable.'

'She would have frightened all the guests.'

'I'm sure with a bit of training Maria will be able to do it.'

Annie had spent the last week hiring waitresses and cleaners, and she was particularly pleased with Maria. She was confident she would be leaving the castle in good hands when she returned to Britain next week.

'Maria is good but she doesn't have the experience and most importantly, she's not you.'

'What do you mean?'

'I'd like to offer you the job of hotel manager, meaning you would live here permanently. Obviously we'd work out extended trips back to Britain to visit Molly, and I'd pay for her to come and stay with you here. What do you think?'

Annie's heart skipped a beat. She would love the job, truly and utterly it was her dream, but she'd already made her decision.

'I'm sorry, Tilly. I don't want to live so far away from Molly. I'm her mum and I know everyone thinks I'm bonkers to go back and live in Britain when I could live here, in this fabulous castle, but I know how hard life is when your mother doesn't live in the same country as you and I don't want that for my daughter.'

'But, darling, you were a child when your parents travelled. Of course you needed them then — but you were there for Molly throughout her childhood. No one could have been a better mum. She's left home, and now it's time for you to have an adventure of your own.'

'I've had an adventure and I've loved

every minute of the last eight months, even the stressful bits, but there's nothing you can say that will change my mind.'

'Nothing I can say, maybe — but I'm betting there's someone here tonight who can.'

Annie's heart sank. She hoped Tilly didn't mean Giovanni. It was unfair of Tilly to expect him to persuade her to stay when she'd already turned him down several times. They'd spoken on the phone a few times but she hadn't seen him since he'd told her he loved her and her heart had broken. She knew he understood why she couldn't stay — and the fact that he didn't argue with her simply made her love him all the more. 'Guests will start arriving soon,' said Tilly.

'You should go and get changed. I'd recommend that lovely dress you bought last week. It looks stunning on you.'

Annie had moved into the staff quarters a fortnight ago, happily giving up the cottage with its tempting location near to Giovanni's farmhouse. The castle was a good twenty-minute walk away from his home. She was far less likely to run down there and throw herself at him if she had too many glasses of wine, which she had been tempted to do a couple of times while staying in the cottage. It wouldn't be fair on him to keep blowing hot and cold on their relationship.

She was pleased with the way the staff quarters had turned out. It was a small space but it felt very homely, and the little bedroom she'd assigned herself was cosy and comfortable. The hotel manager was going to be very happy here.

She'd already planned to wear the maxi dress she'd picked up at the market before Tilly mentioned it. Its blues and greens had caught her eye and so she'd bought it without trying it on, something she never normally did. The gamble had paid off. It had a plunging neckline and then it gathered in at the top of her waist before flowing freely to the ground.

She'd liked it because it showed off the length of her body, which she thought was her best feature. As she brushed her hair, she felt a pang for Molly. Her daughter had a way with hair, which always made Annie feel glamorous whenever she styled hers in an updo.

Her own talents were sadly lacking so she left it loose this evening. It now reached her shoulder blades, which was the longest she'd had it in years, and had developed a slight kink, which she liked to emphasise by scrunching it when it was wet. She was more tanned than she'd ever been in her life so she didn't use much make-up, only brushing a little powder over her nose.

There was a full-length mirror in the hallway. Annie did a little twirl in front of it and was pleased with what she saw. Instead of a drab, middle-aged housewife staring back at her was a woman bursting with possibilities, and she smiled at her reflection.

A future without Giovanni seemed bleak but this project had made her realise she had prospects. Once she returned to Britain she'd find a job that suited her rather than one that just paid the bills.

She was straightening her necklace when a low wolf-whistle sounded. She spun round, recognising the sound of that noise but not daring to believe it was possible.

There, smiling happily at her from the other end of the hallway, was Molly.

'Oh my goodness,' she exclaimed as she rushed down the hall and flung her arms around her daughter. 'What are you doing here?'

'Tilly flew me over as a surprise. She really wanted me to come to your party and to see what a success you've made of her hotel. I have to say, Mum, it looks absolutely stunning. I can't wait for you to show me around properly.'

'Have you got time? Aren't you in the middle of your exams?'

'Mum, don't panic. The exams are over.'

'Already? It's only the beginning of June.'

'Yep, really. I'm all set for a summer of enjoying myself,' said Molly, beaming at her.

Annie couldn't believe they were already done. University was costing a fortune and Molly had only been there a few months — but that didn't matter right now.

'Well, I'm so glad you're here.'

'Me too, Mum. You're looking amazing.' Molly lightly touched Annie's dress. 'This is beautiful.'

'Thank you. What do you think of my hair? I thought I should wear it up but I couldn't manage any of the styles you normally do for me.' 'Leave it down. It suits the outfit and it's so long now it's very pretty.' Molly briefly ran her fingers down the length of it and Annie leaned into her touch, so grateful to have her daughter with her. 'Shall we go and say hello to your guests?'

'Yes, let's. I can't wait to introduce you to everyone. Be prepared for me to be an embarrassing mum.'

Molly laughed and linked arms with her. 'You're always embarrassing. I think that's part of the deal when you become a parent. It's like it's hard-wired into your DNA and there's nothing you can do to stop it.'

Annie nudged her daughter. 'You just wait until it happens to you.'

'I'm fully prepared for it.' Molly laughed. 'Will there be food at this party?' she added, as they made their way up to the main body of the hotel.'

Annie laughed. 'Of course there'll be food — although now that I know you're going to be here I'm not sure we catered enough.'

'I'd best make sure I'm the first one in the queue for the food then,' said Molly smiling.

Annie wasn't sure whether she was joking, Molly did really love food, but Annie didn't really care either way. Annie's insides were fizzing with pleasure. This evening was going to be perfect.

As they reached the lobby Annie's breath caught as she saw Giovanni, in a crisply tailored suit, standing talking to Serena whose arms were around his neck as he held onto her tightly. Even though more of him was covered than usual, the fabric highlighted his strong shoulders and Annie was hit with the urge to run her hands over the hard muscles.

'Isn't that Giovanni Langasco?' whispered Molly.

'Yes — but how do you know that?' asked Annie, turning to her daughter.

'Doesn't everyone know him? He was the face of that holiday company for years, don't you remember the ad campaign? Wow, he's even more gorgeous in the flesh.'

Annie's stomach turned unpleasantly. 'He's too old for you.'

Molly giggled. 'Of course he is, Mum. He must be nearly forty but he's still good-looking for an old guy. I wonder if he'd mind if I took a photo of him. The girls will be well jealous.'

'I think he would mind,' said Annie quickly.

'Yeah, it's probably not a cool thing to do either, is it? Is that his daughter? She's so cute.' Molly had always had a soft spot for young children, which Annie found alarming. She was too young to be a grandmother — although she realised she couldn't very well object. She'd been married and expecting a baby at Molly's age and that had worked out all right.

Her daughter was sensible and mature and she'd have to trust her judgment but still … She didn't want to be a nana before she turned forty.

She was about to point Molly in the direction of the food table when Giovanni spotted her.

'Annie, there you are. I have news.'

'I can't believe you didn't tell me you knew him well enough for him to know your name,' whispered Molly as they made their way over. 'All that time we've chatted on the phone about paint testers and soft furnishings and you didn't mention you know a celebrity.'

'I didn't know he was a celebrity,' Annie whispered b ack. 'I'd never seen him before moving out here. He's just a neighbour.'

'Mmm,' murmured Molly. 'Yes, I can see he's just a neighbour by the way he's looking at you.' Heat rushed up Annie's neck at that comment but there was no time to reassure Molly that nothing was happening because they'd reached him and her heart had started to race uncontrollably.

'This is my daughter, Molly,' said Annie. 'This is Giovanni and his daughter Serena.'

'Hello,' said Molly brightly. 'Shall I take Serena over to the food table so you can tell Mum your news?'

Serena wiggled impatiently at this offer and Giovanni set her down.

'If you don't mind, that would be great. She's been asking for food ever since we got here.'

'It's no trouble at all. Buonasera, Serena. Andiamo.'

Serena smiled up at Molly and slipped her hand into hers as Annie watched them, her mouth slightly ajar.

'I didn't know Molly could speak Italian,' she said, as their daughters disappeared further into the hotel. The rest of the guests followed them until it was only Giovanni and Annie left in the lobby.

'She's certainly doing better than her mother on her first day in Italy,' said Giovanni, grinning.

'Ha, very funny. You'll never, ever let me forget that, will you?'

'Whenever I'm feeling sad I only have to think of you apologising in terrible French and it never fails to bring a smile to my face.'

Annie laughed, 'Well at least now I know I'm good for something. Now tell me what your news is before I explode with the suspense.'

'I heard from the head of the fishing union.'

'And…'

'And … we won.'

'We won! Oh my goodness.' Without thinking she threw her arms around his neck and laughed. 'I can't believe it! What did they say?'

'Apparently Lorenzo and his colleagues were quite easy to persuade when they realised they would lose the backing of the entire fishing union at the next election. They've written a formal letter, which was received today, confirming that permission has been withdrawn for Global Hotel to build anywhere along the coastline around Vescovina. And there's more.'

'Really?'

'Yes, really. Lorenzo rang me earlier.'

'He rang you! Was he obnoxious? Did he yell at you for interfering?'

'No, he was quite pleasant. He offered me the land.'

Annie gasped, 'No way!'

'I'd have to pay for it, of course.'

'Can you afford to?'

'I managed to knock him down a bit but no, I couldn't afford it on my own. However because of Piero's generous donation and all the other small ones, we've got enough. The land can be bought on behalf of all Vescovinians.' He grinned. 'That's going to be a management nightmare in reality, but it sounds good.'

'It sounds amazing. I can't believe it. It's better than I ever hoped. Thank you,

Giovanni, for helping me save this hotel from total ruin.' She reached out and lightly touched his sleeve. 'I can never thank you enough.'

Giovanni covered her hand with his own. 'It's Vescovina that should be thanking you. You didn't give up, and in doing so you've protected an area which is more important to the town than I think any of them realise. And,' he said slowly, 'you won't see the benefit, will you? Carlotta tells me you're returning to Britain next week.'

She nodded, suddenly unable to speak. He squeezed her hand and then let go.

She let go of his sleeve and they stood together, close but not touching.

'I've enjoyed getting to know you, Annie. I hope life brings you many more adventures.'

A lump, the size of a boulder, formed in Annie's throat. She wanted to say so much, but all she could manage was a slight nod.

'Shall we go and join the others? Tilly

tells me there's going to be champagne,' he said, smiling down at her softly.

'Yes,' she croaked.

He turned and Annie followed. Tonight would be the last time she saw him — but she wouldn't be sad. Instead she would rejoice in the friendships she'd made and the happiness knowing him had brought into her life.

24

Fine mist was blowing up from the sea, coating all Annie's belongings in a thin layer of damp. Despite it being the end of June, she was cold.

She'd got used to the Italian climate, and the abrupt change in temperature now she was back in Britain was making her body miserable. But then her mind was miserable too, so at least they matched up.

'Are you sure you want to live here, Mum? It doesn't look very nice,' said Molly, her face scrunched up in disapproval.

'It didn't look bad the day I came to view. It was sunny and the place had a good holiday feel.'

'Well it doesn't any more,' said Molly, carrying a box of books into Annie's new lounge. 'I'm sorry, Mum, but I have to say it looks like a hovel. I feel awful about you moving in here. Can't you come and stay with me for a bit?'

'That's a lovely offer, but you and your friends are going to enjoy living in that flat-share together and I would only cramp your style.'

Molly shook her head.

'You really wouldn't, Mum. We're only going to be working over the summer to pay for next year. It's not as if it will be non-stop partying.'

Annie had to admit that the two-bedroom second-floor flat she'd found overlooking the sea at Witchem Bay was not looking at its best. Tired curtains hung around a grubby window and the carpet seemed far more threadbare than when she'd been shown round the other day. Perhaps a rug had been hiding the worst of the stains — or maybe she'd been too unhappy to even check.

Leaving Giovanni had left her with a hole in her heart that didn't seem to be healing, even after two weeks of trying to get used to the idea. With no other income coming her way for the foreseeable future, Annie had taken this

low-budget flat in order to eke out the wage she'd been paid from Tilly. She didn't want to rush into any old job to pay the bills. This time she was going to find something that suited her — but right now, it felt as though nothing ever would.

She didn't say any of this to Molly.

'The next time you visit, you won't recognise the place,' she said brightly.

'Mum — you do know that I want you to be happy, don't you?'

Annie stilled. Molly's voice was far more serious than she'd ever heard from her daughter before. 'Of course I know that.'

'It's only I'm worried that you're putting me before your own happiness.'

'Well, that's part of being a parent. What's brought this on?'

'Tilly told me that you'd turned down her offer of a job as hotel manager.'

Annie was going to kill Tilly next time she saw her. 'Yes, I did, but that was for a variety of reasons.'

'Which were?'

303

'I ... well, I ...'

'Mum! You loved it out there and anyone with half an eye could tell you and
Giovanni had fallen for each other. I
don't understand why you'd swap that for
this. Tilly said it was because you wanted
to be here for me and that's lovely, but
Italy isn't far away and I'd far rather visit
you in that lovely hotel than in this poor
excuse for a flat.'

'This is only temporary. Once I get a
job I'll be able to afford somewhere better. Now, don't worry about me. Would
you like a cup of tea? I fancy one and
I've unearthed the kettle. I'm sure I put
some tea bags in the yellow box. Could
you put those books in my bedroom?'

She needed to keep moving and being
practical because she was beginning to
suspect Molly was right. She had made
a big mistake. But it was far too late to
put it right.

The buzzer sounded loud and garish
in the silence of the flat.

Molly jumped and dropped the box of
books she was carrying.

'Who can that be? No one knows I'm here,' said Annie, puzzled.

Molly shrugged, although Annie thought the gesture looked forced. 'Probably one of your new neighbours. Either they're going to offer you a bowl of sugar or mug you. It's difficult to tell.'

'Molly — it's a family, seaside resort. Not a drug den.'

'I'll go and answer it and see which one of us is right,' said Molly.

'OK.' Annie made her way into the kitchen. If it was a new neighbour then she may as well get the tea going. She dug around in the yellow box and pulled out tea bags and sugar. Now, where had she left the milk? She knew she hadn't put it in the fridge yet because it needed thoroughly disinfecting.

She heard muffled conversation from the hall, then the sound of Molly letting someone in.

Reflexively, Annie flicked the kettle on.

'Annie, Annie, Annie,' came a high-pitched, excited voice from the lounge.

Annie froze, a tea bag clutched in her hand. It surely couldn't be ...

She made her way into the sitting room.

Sure enough Serena was in Molly's arms, playfully pulling at her hair as she made silly faces at her.

Giovanni was looking impossibly tanned in the washed-out light of the room. Their eyes met. Her knees started shaking uncontrollably.

The power of speech failed her completely. 'There's a park down the road. Shall I take Serena to play there?' Molly asked Giovanni as if this was the most normal situation in the world.

'Mare,' said Serena, pointing imperiously out of the window towards the windswept beach.

'Good idea,' said Molly. 'The beach it is. We'll be back in a bit — and remember, Mum,' said Molly, looking at Annie for the first time since Giovanni had arrived. 'I want you to be happy.'

And with that she left the two of them alone.

Annie opened her mouth to speak and then closed it. She had no idea what to say.

Giovanni slowly looked around the room, the expression on his face unreadable.

'I'd planned this as a big romantic gesture,' he began. 'But now that I am here I'm not sure what to say.'

Annie nodded. Words still seemed to have deserted her.

'I do not think much of your English summer,' he said, glancing at the grey sky outside.

'It was lovely yesterday,' Annie croaked.

Giovanni met her gaze. 'Is this your new flat?'

'It's temporary. It's only somewhere to stay while I find somewhere better.'

'A cardboard box would be better than this.'

'Not all of us have money,' she pointed out.

'True, but some of us could be living in a castle. Instead, one of us is choosing to live here.'

He pushed his hair back from his face, looked down at the carpet and grimaced.

'This floor is a health hazard,' he said, pulling a face.

She let out a surprised giggle. 'It's not good, is it?'

Giovanni reached out a hand to rest it on the back of an armchair. He snatched it back at the last minute when he saw the state of it.

'Annie, don't do this,' he said. 'Come back to Italy. Live with me or live at the castle — but don't settle for this. It's not good enough for you.'

Annie's heart started to pound.

'You're thinking about Molly,' Giovanni stated. Annie nodded.

'Do you know how I knew to come here?' he asked unexpectedly. 'Molly phoned me.'

'She did?'

'Yes. I'm not the only one she's spoken to. She's been on the phone to Carlotta, Tilly — and, I think, even my parents.'

'And she says I'm embarrassing,' said Annie faintly.

Giovanni laughed.

'She wants what's best for you but she also wanted to make sure she'd got it right. It would be awful if she'd persuaded you to return to Italy if none of us wanted you there. But we all do. I do. Molly thinks you'll be happy there with us, and that's all she wants for you.' He took a deep breath and said, less seriously, 'Also, I think she's quite excited about having a famous stepfather.'

Annie didn't know what to make of that. Did Giovanni just propose?

'I didn't actually know you were famous until Molly told me,' she said, settling on that one thing. It was too daunting to be thinking about marriage and all the other things he'd said.

He grinned. 'I know. That's one of the things that makes you so endearing. Also, I spoke to Tilly and she's desperate for you to return to manage the hotel. Apparently all the best ideas were yours and she's snowed under trying to cope with it all and her new hotel at the same time.'

'I see.'

While they'd been talking, they'd moved closer together. Now Annie was close enough to feel the warmth of his breath across her cheek.

'Molly seems to adore Serena, so that's a good start,' she murmured.

'Mmm, yes, I'm only in this for the free babysitting opportunities,' he said, threading his fingers through hers and pulling her close.

Their bodies were touching and Annie could see his pulse beating wildly in his neck. Her own was racing too.

'So what's it to be?' he whispered. 'Italy with its deep-blue sky, endless sun, crystal blue sea and me... or this?'

'Well, I am really missing the sun...' she said. He laughed, and she kissed him. She was going home.

We do hope that you have enjoyed reading this large print book.

Did you know that all of our titles are available for purchase?

We publish a wide range of high quality large print books including:
Romances, Mysteries, Classics
General Fiction
Non Fiction and Westerns

Special interest titles available in large print are:
The Little Oxford Dictionary
Music Book, Song Book
Hymn Book, Service Book

Also available from us courtesy of Oxford University Press:
Young Readers' Dictionary
(large print edition)
Young Readers' Thesaurus
(large print edition)

For further information or a free brochure, please contact us at:
Ulverscroft Large Print Books Ltd.,
The Green, Bradgate Road, Anstey,
Leicester, LE7 7FU, England.
Tel: (00 44) 0116 236 4325
Fax: (00 44) 0116 234 0205

Other titles in the
Linford Romance Library:

A BODY IN THE CHAPEL

Philippa Carey

Ipswich, 1919: On her way to teach Sunday School, Margaret Preston finds a badly injured man unconscious at the chapel gate. She and her widowed father, Reverend Preston, take him in and call the doctor. When the stranger regains consciousness, he tells them he has lost his memory, not knowing who he is or how he came to be there. As he and Margaret grow closer, their fondness for one another increases. But she is already being courted by another man ...

BLETCHLEY SECRETS

Dawn Knox

1940: A cold upbringing with parents who unfairly blame her for a family tragedy has robbed Jess of all self-worth and confidence. Escaping to join the WAAF, she's stationed at RAF Holsmere, until a seemingly unimportant competition leads to her recruitment into the secret world of code-breaking at Bletchley Park. Love, however, eludes her: the men she chooses are totally unsuitable – until she meets Daniel. But there is so much which separates them. Can they ever find happiness together?

THE LOMBARDI EMERALDS

Margaret Mounsdon

Who is Auguste Lombardi, and why has May's mother been invited to his eightieth birthday party? As her mother is halfway to Australia, and May is resting between acting roles, she attends in her place. To celebrate the occasion, she wears the earrings her mother gave her for her birthday – only to discover that they are not costume jewellery, but genuine emeralds, and part of the famous missing Lombardi collection ...